Luke could feel his insides twisting up, and in his fury he wanted to hit someone. He tried to get around Isabelle, but the agent grabbed him.

"*Luke!* Get control of yourself!" she ordered.

"How far away is it?" Through his rage Luke heard the worry in Adam's voice and saw he was on his cell phone. Behind him, Luke could see that people were pouring out of the buildings. A group of Marines started jogging up the main road.

"What's going on, Adam?" Isabelle asked.

Adam snapped his phone shut. "The forest fire east of here is spreading."

WILDFIRE RUN

DEE GARRETSON

HARPER

An Imprint of HarperCollinsPublishers

Wildfire Run

www.harpercollinschildrens.com

Library of Congress Cataloging-in-Publication Data

Garretson, Dee.

Wildfire run / Dee Garretson. — 1st ed.

p.   cm.

Summary: A relaxing retreat to Camp David turns deadly after a faraway earthquake sets off a chain of disastrous events that trap the president's twelve-year-old son, Luke, and his two friends within the compound.

ISBN 978-0-06-195350-7

[1. Presidents—Family—Fiction.   2. Camp David (Md.)—Fiction.
3. Earthquakes—Fiction.   4. Forest fires—Fiction.   5. Survival—
Fiction.   6. Adventures and adventurers—Fiction.]   I. Title.

PZ7.G18443Wi   2010   2009049482
[Fic]—dc22   CIP
                                                                  AC

Typography by Larissa Lawrynenko
12 13 14 15   CG/BR   10 9 8 7 6 5 4 3
❖
First paperback edition, 2011

For my father, Keith Garretson,
who would have seen himself and his
influence in many parts of this story

Contents

1

Meramec River, Missouri

The roar came from deep in the earth, growing louder as it raced toward the surface. Within seconds the river began to tremble. Fish, only a few at first, then more and more, leaped out of the water, slapping back down onto it with sharp claps. As the earthquake struck, the land jolted violently. The ground heaved. Shock waves radiated out in all directions, spreading fast, shaking everything in their path.

2

Camp David

The helicopter hovered two feet above Theo's nose. The tiny rotors were buzzing, but Theo didn't stir, didn't open his eyes. He just kept sleeping. Luke, sitting cross-legged on his own bed with the remote control, moved the lever a fraction. The helicopter dropped down just enough so that the feather dangling from it brushed his friend's forehead. Still no reaction.

Except from Comet, Luke's dog, who jumped up on the bed, whining and bumping his arm. The helicopter took a dive, nearly crashing into

Theo's thick, curly hair. Luke pulled the lever back just in time. If the helicopter had gone into that hair, it would have been a goner, like one of those prehistoric creatures sucked down into a tar pit and turned into a fossil.

"Comet, stop, please, I need to concentrate. I'll get up in just a minute." Still whining, the Jack Russell terrier circled around Luke. The bed began to shake. It made no sense. How could a small dog like Comet shake a big piece of furniture?

Luke tried to get up, but the floor shifted under him and he lost control, crashing the helicopter. On the other side of the room, the electric train table shook, and the railcars slid sideways into the wall. The trestle bridge shivered as a tiny plastic cow grazing in a pasture fell onto the track. Luke couldn't take his eyes off the cow wobbling back and forth in front of the train.

A siren blared outside and his mouth went dry, panic taking over. Adam Martens, one of Luke's Secret Service agents, opened the door as Comet dove under the bed.

"Luke, stand still," Adam ordered.

Luke managed one gulp of air. "What's happening? What do we need to do?"

"Relax. Look at me. Take a deep breath. It's an earthquake."

"An earthquake! Where's my dad?" Luke was already moving to the window to see if his father was in the pool for his morning swim.

"Stay away from the window until the shaking stops," Adam ordered, but Luke was already there, holding the sill to steady himself. He could see his dad in the deep end, swimming toward the edge of the pool as waves sloshed out, drenching two Secret Service agents who knelt on the ground trying to reach his father.

The shaking stopped and the siren cut off abruptly. Luke watched the agents help his dad out of the pool, surrounding him as they moved toward the lodge.

"Look, he's fine," Adam said as he came over to Luke. "A minor earthquake isn't going to faze the President of the United States."

"That was pretty weird." Luke relaxed. "I've never been in an earthquake before. I can't believe Theo slept through it all."

The outside door to the lodge opened, and Luke heard his father's voice in the hall. "Is it confirmed? I have to get to the situation room; there should be reports already coming in. If we felt it all the way here, the damage must be horrendous." His father's tone was calm as always, but Luke knew that didn't mean anything. His father never sounded upset, so it was impossible for Luke to ever judge when something was really wrong.

"Sir, I think we should stay outside until we know the full extent of the quake." Luke couldn't tell which agent spoke. "There may be aftershocks."

"No, absolutely not. I'm not going to overreact to a small amount of shaking. Camp David is eight hundred miles from the epicenter. We're perfectly safe here."

3

Camp Misty Mount

The sign posted at the entrance to the campground read, NO CAMPFIRES, EXTREME FIRE DANGER. A park ranger had put up the sign two weeks earlier, when the drought entered its third month, turning the dead leaves and brush to perfect tinder.

Sam Trent's family was almost ready to leave. The day before, all fifty-one of his cousins and aunts and uncles had gone off to their homes in three different states.

"Check the fire pit one more time, Sam," Michael Trent told his son, putting the last bag in the car. They hadn't been able to resist building just one fire to roast marshmallows the night before they left. It wouldn't be a Trent family outing without marshmallows. They had been very careful, pouring water on the ashes before they went to bed.

Sam poked through the ashes with a stick. The fire pit wasn't really a pit; it was just a ring of stones on a bare patch of ground in front of cabin number three. The ashes in the middle were still clumped together from the water the night before, but on the edge of the pit Sam uncovered some embers they had missed.

"It's still going, Dad," he yelled.

"Pour another bucket of water on it. Hurry, we need to get on the road if we're going to make it home today."

Sam propped the stick up on one of the rocks, eager to go home. It was kind of creepy being the last ones left, surrounded by all the quiet in the woods.

The end of the stick started to glow, but Sam didn't notice. It took him only a minute to get some more water, and three minutes later they were all off in the car.

One squirrel chased another up on the porch of

cabin six, but both stopped in midrun as if playing freeze tag. The earthquake tremors started a millisecond later. The cabins, built of chestnut planks, wavered on their stone pilings, but settled back in place. The stick wobbled, and then fell off its prop, down onto one dry leaf.

The leaf burned in an instant, catching another leaf, until there was a circle of fire spreading outward in all directions. Slowly the thin layer of leaves on the ground caught fire, sparking for an instant like fallen fireflies, each leaf burning out quickly just as another one caught.

The squirrels, catching a whiff of the smoke, ran into the woods. A deer chewing on the bark of a sapling lifted her head, looking at the flames. When the fire reached the edge of the road and found a larger pile of leaves, it flamed, burning eagerly. The doe bounded off to the west, toward Camp David.

4

Nelson Residence

"Be patient, Ralph, and you'll get fed too." The collie thumped his tail as Liz Nelson put the bacon in the hot skillet. The bacon sizzled and little bits of hot grease jumped about in the pan. "Maybe I'll even give you some bacon, since I have to go in to school today." Liz taught fifth grade at Thurmont Elementary, and with school starting soon it was time to get her classroom back in order.

She was just debating whether to hang the solar system decorations or the fall leaf cutouts when the house began to shake. The old farmhouse wavered back and forth as if a giant held it, rattling it as if it were a piggy bank. Liz fell toward the stove, trying to catch herself on the counter. Her left arm bumped the skillet, pushing it off the flames, spattering the sparking grease over the stove and into the wastebasket next to it. Liz couldn't move her arm back in time and the flames came up around it.

She screamed, jumping back, and Ralph barked at the stove as if under attack. Running to the sink, Liz turned the faucet on, letting the cold water pour over the scorched skin, tears welling up in her eyes.

Through the pain, she didn't see the flaming bit of grease catch on a paper towel in the wastebasket.

The collie came over and pressed close against her.

"It's okay, Ralph." Liz turned off the water and examined her arm. The blisters covered both sides. "I think I need to go to the emergency room, buddy. I wish you could drive me." She turned off the stove and grabbed the car keys off the holder by the back door.

"Come on, Ralph. You stay outside until I get back." By the time the car pulled out of the driveway, the paper towel was aflame, breaking into pieces. A gust of wind blew in through the window above the sink, sending a bit of burning paper into the curtains of the window above the table. One caught fire. Within four minutes, the rest of the kitchen began to burn. Ralph stood outside, paws on the windowsill, barking, but because the nearest neighbor was a quarter mile away and the back of the farmhouse bordered the woods of Catoctin Mountain Park, no one heard.

5

The Presidential Lodge

The sirens blasted again, and then shut off.

"Why did they go off? What's wrong? Should we—" Luke stopped himself before Adam could hear the quavering in his voice. Luke hated the sirens. They were supposed to sound only in a real emergency, and he had imagined too many different emergencies to ever be able to ignore the noise. The fear usually sat in the back of Luke's head, a dark, solid lump he couldn't ignore. He didn't want Adam or anyone else to know how much he worried about terrorists and all the horrible things they could do to him, but he suspected Adam, at least, knew anyway.

"There's nothing to worry about," Adam said, tapping his earpiece. "The earthquake probably caused some minor problems with the sensors. If there were anything wrong, I would have heard about it already."

Adam always said "don't worry," but he was paid to worry. Once when Luke was six, he was watching his dad give a campaign speech at a county fair. A crazy person came out of the crowd, running with his hands outstretched and his fingers curled as if he was going to strangle Luke. An agent tackled the man and put handcuffs on him before Luke even understood what was happening. While the crowd went crazy, Adam picked Luke up and carried him away to the car, ignoring the chaos around them, telling Luke not to worry the whole time.

Now that Luke was twelve, and his dad was President, he knew his mom and dad worried about not just crazy people, but about terrorists who could take him to force his dad to do something terrible.

It was the main reason Luke loved Camp David. A mile of woods in every direction protected them from the outside world. To Luke, the fences were like a high-tech moat. Two fences, one of them electric, separated the woods from the national park outside the boundary. The outer fence was wooden, posted with signs to warn about the real barricade, the electric fence pulsing with enough charge to stop any terrorists from getting inside. As long as he was inside the fences, nothing could get to him.

Luke knelt down to pet Comet. For some reason, running his hand through the dog's wiry white coat always made him feel better.

"Is Theo still asleep or is he just faking?" Adam asked. Theo hadn't moved an inch, as far as Luke could tell.

"He's asleep. He sleeps through anything, I think. I was just doing some experiments to see what would wake him up." Luke got up and recovered the helicopter, feeling some of the tension go away. If Adam wasn't hearing anything bad through his earpiece, nothing *was* wrong.

Adam admired the feather on the string. "Clever," he said. "Reminds me of the time my sister was sleeping and I put a piece of tissue over her mouth to see if it would stop her snoring. You should have heard her scream when she woke up. She thought it was a moth."

"Sweet." Luke glanced at Theo.

"Wait a minute," Adam said, laughing. "That wasn't a suggestion."

Too worked up to keep still, Luke beat out a djembe drum rhythm on the edge of the train table.

"Hey, it's still early. Why don't you let him sleep and we can go for a run," Adam said.

"Can we race? Sprints?" All the agents were in great shape, but Adam was the only one willing to race him, and getting outside sounded good.

"You just like to win, don't you?"

"Who doesn't?" Luke said, grinning. Even though Adam could beat him at a distance, sometimes Luke outran him over short spans. "I'll be dressed in just a minute. Who's on duty with you?" The agents usually worked in teams of two.

"Isabelle today," Adam said.

Luke liked to tease Isabelle. She was so serious it was a challenge to get her to smile. "Tell her she needs the exercise," he suggested.

"You tell her. If I say that, I'll be on the ground before I can blink."

"Chicken," Luke said. He knew Adam was just kidding. He'd been an Army Ranger before he joined the Secret Service, and Luke doubted if anyone could throw a Ranger to the ground.

"Everybody's a chicken when it comes to Isabelle. She's pretty tough. Come on, get dressed. I'll let her know the plan." Adam walked out, shutting the door behind him.

"Comet, you want to go for a run?" Luke asked, discarding his pajamas and pulling on his clothes. At the word "run," the dog jumped up. Luke was sure Comet knew what "run" meant. Comet might not obey a lot of the time, but he was smart. Sort of smart, Luke corrected himself, as Comet picked up Luke's sneaker and carried it under the bed.

Luke wrestled back the shoe and finished dressing. His locator disk flashed in the mirror, and he tucked it out of sight under his shirt. The Secret Service monitored him constantly, and they insisted that he wear the GPS disk at all times. Luke hated wearing the thing, but whenever he tried to leave it off, an agent soon told him to put it back on. It was like having a baby monitor around his neck. So far Theo hadn't noticed it, though. Luke supposed he would have to explain the disk when they went swimming.

Still no motion from Theo, which was okay,

because he wasn't much for exercise. Luke hadn't known Theo for very long, but he had already figured that out. Theo was one of the smartest people he had ever met. Luke had joined the robotics club at school late in the spring, and he and Theo had hit it off right away. Theo didn't seem to care that Luke's dad was the President. He treated Luke just like everybody else, telling Luke when he was putting something together the wrong way, even telling Luke he thought his jokes weren't very good. They weren't, but no one else ever said so. Most of the other kids at school all laughed their heads off, like he was the funniest person on the planet.

The window rattled, startling him. Luke held still, waiting to see if the room would shake again, but nothing happened.

Out in the hall, Adam was talking to Christine Cooper, one of his dad's assistants. Luke didn't know what her official title was, but he thought of her as the timekeeper. She followed his dad around, reminding him of what he had to do, checking her watch so many times a day Luke was sure her arm moved up and down automatically even when she wasn't working.

"Good morning, Luke," Christine said. "I was

just telling Adam your father wants to have lunch with you. I've put it on his schedule."

"Why?" Luke was surprised. Even though they were supposed to be on vacation, he usually saw his dad only at dinner, and there were always other people around.

"He wants to check on how you're getting along with your summer reading list for school."

"Oh." It figured there was a practical reason, and it would just happen to be about something Luke hadn't done. His dad wouldn't be happy to find out Luke hadn't finished reading any of the books.

"Lunch is scheduled for twelve thirty. Don't be late." Christine was already walking away, checking her watch.

Luke turned to Adam. He'd worry about the books later. "Are we cleared to go now?"

"Sorry, pal." Adam tapped his earpiece again, listening with a frown. "I was just told we're supposed to stay put for a while. They have to run checks on all the sensor systems because of the earthquake, just to make sure everything is working correctly."

"You mean we're stuck inside all day? I wanted to show Theo the tree house and then the garage, and once we get the robot put together, we want to try it outside." Luke had made a real effort to keep his hands off his new robot kit until Theo could help assemble it.

"We'll be able to go outside as soon as they're done with the inner zone," Adam said. Luke knew the inner zone was a circle consisting of most of the buildings in the center of the camp. "They'll test the outer zone in the woods all the way to the fences after that. Maybe we can go for a run on the nature trail when that section is clear."

"Great," Luke said glumly. He took Comet back to his bedroom, slamming the door behind them.

"What's going on?" Theo asked. He sat up and felt around on his nightstand for his glasses. "Why are you up so early?" His hair sprang up in a fan around the top of his head, out of control.

"Did you know when you wake up you look like a bergruutfa caravan beast?" Luke asked. Theo wouldn't be able to top that one.

Theo put on his glasses and peered at Luke. "You shouldn't talk about hair. If those bits of hair that stick up on the top of your head were green instead of almost albino blond, you would make a perfect reptilian Rodian. Maybe you could just

19

be an albino Rodian. I'm going back to sleep." Theo took his glasses off, lay down, and then sat up again. "I don't remember what planet the bergruutfa caravan beasts come from."

"Ha!" Luke was thrilled. It wasn't often he knew more about *Star Wars* than Theo. "Teloc Ol-sen," he said, trying to smooth down the cowlicks. Theo was right, unfortunately; they did look like Rodian antennae.

"Now I'm awake," Theo said. "You never answered me. Why are you up so early?"

"Everybody but you is up, because there was an earthquake. You slept through it all. It was a long way away, so we only felt some shaking—but there were sirens."

Adam knocked on the door and then came in. "Morning, Theo. Luke, since we can't go for a run now, why don't you boys have breakfast?"

The window rattled again, harder this time, and Luke looked around for something to steady himself, in case it was another earthquake.

"It's just the wind," Adam said. "The forecast is for high winds all day, but no storms. Nothing to worry about."

6

The Command Center

The Marines in the underground command center at Camp David knew they were sitting under twenty-one thousand gallons of water, but they never worried about it, assuming whoever built the President's pool knew what they were doing.

But, in fact, when then President Richard Nixon decided he wanted a new pool outside the back porch of his lodge, no one spoke up to tell him the site was a poor choice. It was right over the main security operations room of the command center, which was based in what had originally been a small bomb shelter. The roof of that room had to be reinforced to support the weight of the new pool's water. An outside entrance to the bomb shelter and the concrete steps leading underground were covered over for a new pool house.

Crumbled bedrock like that in California damps down earthquake waves, preventing them from spreading too far, but the bedrock between the pool's bottom and the security operations room's ceiling was in large slabs, like most of the bedrock east of the Mississippi. When the earth-quake struck in Missouri, the waves spreading east didn't have much to slow them down, and the strong waves traveled thousands of miles.

Six minutes after the quake, the swimming pool in Maryland shifted slightly, cracking the concrete on the bottom.

When the shaking of the earth stopped and the agents rushed the President inside, no one realized that pool water had begun to seep down through the crack.

As the water trickled down, it spread out, find-ing a groove in the bedrock. The groove angled farther down and the water became a tiny stream pulled along by gravity, until it came to the edge of the slab. The stream couldn't jump across to the next slab, so it dripped into the space between the two rocks, continuing its downward path. The drips found a level spot and formed a puddle on the ceiling panels above the security operations room. Only the size of a dime at first, the puddle grew with each passing minute.

7

The Situation Room

Luke was embarrassed that he let a little wind bother him. "I knew it wasn't anything," he told Theo. "Let's find out what's happening with the earthquake before we have breakfast. Maybe Dad will let us go to the situation room. I'll be right back." Luke darted out the door and down the hall to his father's room.

"Dad!" he called.

His father, still in his wet swim trunks, stood surrounded by a group of people in suits. Sometimes it seemed as if all the people around his father never slept; they were always following him with briefing papers to read, speeches to go over, or information his dad had to know right then, no matter what he was doing. Luke wasn't stupid; he knew being the President meant his dad needed all those people, but most of the time they felt like a concrete wall to keep him out.

"Scientists have been predicting a quake at the New Madrid fault for years. I just wish they'd been wrong," his father said, drying his hair with a towel.

"Dad, can we come with you to the sit. room?" Luke asked when he reached his father's side. Luke wasn't allowed in the real situation room at the White House very often, because it was full of people busy monitoring world events, but his dad took him into the one at Camp David once in a while, mostly to show him places on the computer maps.

"Yes, get dressed," Luke's father said without even looking at him, not noticing he was already dressed. Luke could see the creases in his father's forehead deepen as he read the piece of paper in his hand. Pierce Brockett was only fifty, but four years as Vice President and two as President had lined his face and turned his hair so gray he looked more like a grandfather than a father. If he won reelection and they were all stuck in the White House for another four years, Luke dreaded to think how old his father would look at the end.

President Brockett's lips moved without any sound, and Luke knew what his father was saying. Pierce Brockett once told Luke that when a crisis happened, he always thought of the words, "Yield not to misfortunes, but rather go more boldly to meet them." It was one of the many ancient Latin sayings his dad loved, like he loved all ancient things. When Theo and Luke's dad started talking, the two would go on and on about ancient philosophy and ancient Romans and pretty much ancient anything. Luke tuned in only if they got on ancient battles or inventions.

His father turned and moved away, the crowd of people moving too, matching his motions just the way a flock of birds followed the leader.

"Did you hear, Adam? Dad says we can go to the situation room."

"I heard, but remind Theo to get dressed. I don't think anyone has ever shown up there in pajamas."

Luke hurried to his room. Theo was still in bed, drawing in his notebook. He carried a notebook with him everywhere, sketching designs and making lists, checking things off, always with some little stub of a pencil. Luke couldn't remember ever seeing him without it.

"Theo, if you get dressed, we can go see what's happening with my dad."

"Okay," Theo said. "Comet isn't happy. He keeps whining."

"Hey, boy, you're going to have to come out sometime, you know." Luke tried to coax the dog out from under the bed by patting the floor and wiggling his fingers.

"Maybe there will be another earthquake," Theo said. "Animals are supposed to be able to sense them coming." He scribbled a few more lines. "If we're going to make the robot with the grabber arm, I think we should program it so we can control its movements by the sound sensor. The light sensor wouldn't work very well outside in the sunlight. . . ."

"Theo, this was a big earthquake," Luke said, "in some place called New Madrid, really big. I want to see what's happening. My dad says we can go to the situation room."

"You mean the New Madrid fault? That's in Missouri. There was a giant earthquake there in 1812." Luke should have realized Theo would know exactly where and what New Madrid was. If it involved disasters, Theo knew everything, even down to things like the name of the captain of the *Titanic*, and how fast the Great Chicago Fire spread.

Theo started getting dressed, talking excitedly the whole time. "It even changed the course of the Mississippi River so that people thought it was running backward. Whole sections of forest were swallowed up."

Luke tried to imagine forests sinking beneath the ground, but it was hard to picture. Did a giant crevice open up just long enough to swallow the forests and then close over them? He started to ask Theo and then he stopped. Theo would launch into a complicated explanation, and Luke's dad might not stay in the situation room for very long.

By the time Theo was dressed and they went out in the hallway, it was empty except for Adam and Isabelle. Luke had a whole detail of his own agents. They even went to school with him, one standing out in the hall while he was in class, and one sitting in the back of the room. At Camp David, their job was to follow him around, so when Luke and Theo headed for the sit. room,

Adam and Isabelle trailed after them:

Theo whispered, "Why is Adam wearing a fishing vest? Are we going fishing?"

"No," Luke said, "that's where he keeps his gun. At Camp David it looks silly if they follow me around wearing suit jackets. Dad's agents almost always wear suits, though."

"Oh." Theo didn't say anything else, and Luke hoped he was okay with being watched. He wanted Theo to like Camp David so he would want to come back.

"Part of the command center used to be a bomb shelter," Luke said as they went down the back stairs. "My dad told me people used to be really afraid back when Russia was the Soviet Union that they would bomb us. People even built bomb shelters in their backyards. Pretty crazy, don't you think?"

"Yeah," Theo said. "I wonder what happened to them all? It would be amazing to have one you could turn into an underground laboratory."

When they reached the locked door at the bottom of the stairs, Adam came around Luke, pushed an intercom button, and spoke into it: "Three eight one." The lock clicked and then the door opened. An agent stood on the other side.

"Morning, Dan," Adam said. "We'll be back this way shortly."

"I'll be here," the man answered.

About twenty feet down the hall, the corridor split left and right. Luke pointed to the hallway to the right. "This way," he said. Hector, a Marine guard who was one of Luke's friends, stood outside a door.

"I'm sorry," Hector said when they reached him. "I'm not authorized to let your buddy inside." Hector looked so apologetic Luke knew he felt bad. Most of the Marine guards were good guys. Hector and some of the others even played basketball with Luke when they were off duty, but when they were on duty they never bent the rules. Camp David was officially a Navy facility, which was funny because the ocean was nowhere near them. Luke knew the Marines liked to be assigned there, so they weren't going to do anything to get sent away.

It was stupid they wouldn't just let Theo in, though, as if he were going to blab some top-secret information. Luke wished he could show Theo the security ops down the hall, but he knew only his father could get Theo in there, and today his dad would be too busy. It was full of computers and screens showing all the views of Camp David from the security cameras. Luke liked it because it looked like the inside of a bridge on a spaceship.

"Let me see about Theo." Adam pushed the intercom button and spoke into it. A few minutes later one of the agents on the presidential detail opened the door to let them all in. Everyone was staring at the television screen on the wall. Luke maneuvered around until he was close enough to see. A newscaster who'd interviewed his dad at the White House was on screen standing in front of a map of the United States.

"A major earthquake hit Missouri a few minutes ago, at five forty-one a.m., central time. The damage reports are already coming in from all over the state. Buildings in St. Louis and other towns have collapsed and several fires have broken out. Here's an eyewitness video just in from a resident of Burlington, Missouri."

The video showed piles of bricks and debris along a road, with parts of cars sticking up from beneath the rubble. The view jumped to a twisted sign that read, ANGIE'S CAFÉ. It took Luke a second to realize he was seeing a small-town main street. Police and ambulance sirens blared in the background, and a woman with blood pouring down the side of her face ran across the screen. She was screaming and crying at the same time. Luke turned away, feeling shaky.

"We'll have to get back to the White House," Luke's dad said, and immediately people began to move about.

Luke stepped up to him quickly. "Dad, can Theo and I stay here?" If his dad made them go with him, they'd just sit around in the residence quarters at the White House with nothing to do while his dad was in endless meetings.

"What? Mark, I want to do a flyover as soon as possible, if it won't disrupt rescue efforts."

"Can Theo and I stay here?" Luke tried to get his father's attention again. "When you and Mom are on trips I stay at the White House without you, so can we stay here?"

Pierce Brockett's chief of staff came over. "Mr. President, the governor of Missouri is calling."

Luke's dad took the phone. "Fine, Luke, you can stay as long as George and Sal okay it. Get Adam to clear it." Luke's hopes sank. George Michelson was the head of the whole White House Secret Service detail, and Salvatorio Rossi was in charge of Luke's detail. Both of them said no to most things Luke wanted to do.

If anyone could convince them, though, it would be Adam. Surely Adam would much rather stay at Camp David than go back to the White House. If they went back, Adam would just have to stand around inside too. When they were at Camp David and Adam was on duty, Luke could tinker around in the grounds maintenance garage, where the tools and trucks and golf carts and lawn mowers were kept. Adam wasn't allowed to help Luke take apart or put together anything, because agents were supposed to keep their hands free, but he could offer advice and explain things, and Luke could get as dirty and greasy as he wanted. Some days Luke even got to drive the golf carts. Luke hoped Theo would like working in the garage too. He worried it wouldn't seem so great to a kid who got to do normal stuff.

"Adam, do you think you can convince Sal and George to let us stay?" Luke said, going over to Adam. Adam stood next to Theo by the back wall, both of them absorbed by the TV.

"What?" It took Adam a moment to take his eyes off the screen.

"My dad says Theo and I can stay if Sal and

George okay it. Can you talk to them? I really want to stay."

"I'll give it a shot. Why don't we go to the dining room, and while you two have some breakfast I'll talk to Sal."

Now that Adam had mentioned breakfast again, Luke realized he was hungry. He felt like he shouldn't be thinking about food in the middle of a disaster, but he couldn't help it.

"Theo, are you hungry?" Luke asked.

"I'm starving," Theo said.

"Sir, reports coming in indicate the earthquake was so large, multiple states are affected," another aide said.

Luke looked back at the television, the screen now showing a huge building on fire. He turned to go, hoping everyone had gotten out safely.

8

Cabin Four

The fire took its time at first, flaring in spots with heavy underbrush, burning twigs and leaves and dead plants. In other spots it almost died out, in areas swept bare by human traffic. The first cabin to catch, strangely, was not cabin number three. The fire couldn't find anything to consume in the bare earth in front of the building, so it headed in another direction. The wind carried it forward.

Cabin four caught first. A pile of sticks left behind provided the fuel, and the fire burned them greedily. Sparks flew up, catching on some of the rough siding of the cabin. As the sparks started tiny individual fires on the siding, each looked like a glowing star in a miniature universe. Soon, though, the whole side of the building was aflame, and as it burned, new sparks flew off in the gusting wind, seeking fresh sources of fuel.

Minutes later, the doe, still running, burst upon three more of her kind who were milling about, unsure what to do. The three could already smell the smoke. Seeing the flight of one of their own, they knew the fire was close. When the doe ran by, they followed.

9

Hagerstown Motel

"Dad, you don't even have to start work until tomorrow. Why do we have to get there so early today?" Only minutes after the earthquake, Callie's dad had rushed her down to the motel parking lot to wait for their ride to Camp David.

"I want us to have the whole day to get settled, and ease my way in with the Navy chef. I don't know how he will feel about my taking over his kitchen for the next week."

Callie knew her dad was excited. Back at the President's ranch in Colorado, his chef talents went mostly unused. The President and his family didn't get there much anymore, just once or twice a year. The new job as the President's assistant chef was such a big promotion, her dad said he would be crazy not to take it.

When he told her about it, Callie was mad enough to scream. She didn't want to leave her horse, Hania, or her dog, Kele, and the ranch where she had lived all her life, for a city and a school full of kids she didn't know. After days of arguing, they settled on a compromise: Callie would go to Camp David for the week, and then start school in Washington, D.C. If she hated it, and she knew she would, her dad had promised she could go back to the ranch and stay with her aunt Kate, the President's housekeeper.

"When you see the First Lady, remember to thank her for arranging for you to come with me."

"I will," Callie said, adjusting the backpack on her shoulder and grabbing her jacket. She knew the First Lady felt sorry for her because her mom had died, even though Callie couldn't even remember her mom. Mrs. Brockett always smiled and looked so perfect, it was scary. She wore dresses all the time, and high heels and makeup. Callie thought she should feel sorry for the First Lady, not the other way around.

Callie twisted her braid, wishing she had pinned it up off her neck. It was already too hot. Her hair was straight and shiny black, and she hoped the single braid made her look more Hopi than she really was, only one-quarter Native American. At least she was something interesting, more than Luke Brockett, whatever he was besides blond and rich.

It was hard to remember now how they had been best friends when they were little kids, back when Luke lived at the ranch. Last time he visited, he had hardly talked to her. All he wanted to do was play some online space game. She finally convinced him to go riding, and even let him ride Hania, but then he had fallen off the horse and yelled at her when she laughed. She hadn't really been laughing at him; she was laughing at the look on Hania's face. The horse looked like she had planned to make Luke fall off.

The Secret Service agents got mad at Callie too. She didn't know Luke wasn't supposed to ride unless one of the agents went along. After he got up off the ground, he had just stomped off like he was some sort of royalty while an agent lectured her. They hadn't spoken since. Callie checked her pocket for the rock she had brought from home. It was a silvery galena, the shiniest she had ever found. If Luke was back to acting normal, she might just give it to him. Even he would be impressed by it.

"I thought you said it was green in the mountains," Callie said as an ovenlike breeze hit her face. Her dad always made it sound as if anything east of the Mississippi was some sort of paradise, but the grass and trees were almost as brown as the plants around the ranch in the summer.

"Must be the heat spell. Camp David is higher up. It will be greener there," her dad said. "Didn't Aunt Kate buy you some sneakers to wear instead of your cowboy boots?" Her dad pointed at her red ostrich-print boots. "I don't know anything about fashion, but I don't think kids out east wear cowboy boots, especially not with shorts."

Callie looked down at her boots. They were just a little scruffy, but they were broken in and comfortable. "She did, but I like these better."

"I just want you to make some friends at your new school."

"What do cowboy boots have to do with that?"

"Nothing, I guess." Her dad gave her braid a little tug.

Callie heard a faint squeak from under one of

the bushes. She looked down and saw a small kitten crouched on the ground. It was black all over, fluffy, soft kitten fuzz. Even its whiskers were black. The only color came from its blue-green eyes.

"Hey, you, what's wrong?" Callie reached down through the leaves and picked up the kitten. It was so small, it couldn't have been more than five or six weeks old. It hissed and bit her finger with little teeth hardly sharper than a pencil point.

"Calm down, tough guy. Dad, look, I found a kitten." She held it up.

"The mother is probably close by," he said, busy scanning the parking lot for the car. "Put it back where you found it."

"But, Dad, the poor thing is so skinny. I think it's lost. Can I keep him?"

"No! You can't take a kitten to Camp David. Go give him to the lady at the reception desk. She'll do something with him."

"Okay," Callie said, knowing it was useless to argue with him.

"I'll wait out here," he said. "Take the kitten inside, but hurry."

When Callie opened the door to the lobby, she saw a woman with blond pouffy hair talking on the phone. The woman wore too much pink lipstick and she had squinty eyes. She looked like a cat hater.

The woman didn't notice her. The kitten mewed again and started to lick Callie's hand. It was so little the scratchy tongue felt like a tickle. Callie looked back to the entrance. Her dad was turned toward the parking lot. She pulled her jacket on and put the kitten in the pocket, closing her hand around its little body.

"Be quiet now and everything will be all right," Callie whispered as she went back outside.

10

Catoctin Mountain Park

The gusting wind confused the deer. The smell of the smoke came from too many different directions, and they didn't know which way to run. They turned to the north. A bear, rooting for grubs in a fallen log, saw them. Sniffing the air, he shifted his head from side to side, and the scent of the fire came to him. He started after the deer, then stopped, knowing that way would take him too close to humans. He headed toward his den, craving its safety.

11

Temporary Haven

In the dining room, Luke poured the maple syrup over his pancake until the syrup ran over the edges and covered the plate.

"That's a lot of syrup," Theo said. "My mom would have a harpy fit if she saw that. She's on a major no-sugar kick."

"It's maple syrup, not sugar. Besides, your mom's not here. Take as much as you want." They were by themselves, surrounded by enough pancakes and sausages and eggs and pastries for ten people. Luke's dad and everybody else were too busy to eat.

Theo held the syrup bottle up high and poured a stream down, not quite covering his entire pancake. "It looks like a giant blob engulfing a planet." He picked up his fork and stabbed at the syrup at different spots on the plate.

"Planet destruction commencing." Luke stuffed a big bite into his mouth. "Wait until Chef Lansa gets here. His pancakes are even better than these."

"Oh, you mean that girl's dad. Is she going to follow us around all the time, or will we be able to do stuff without her?" Theo asked.

Luke groaned. "I don't think she's going to want to hang around us much." He wished his mom hadn't arranged for Callie to come. His mom didn't know they had stopped being friends. Last time he saw Callie at the ranch, she purposely teased him to get up on that crazy horse and then laughed when the horse tried to brush him off against the fence. He wouldn't have fallen off if he hadn't been trying to keep his leg from being squashed. Callie probably taught the horse to do that herself. Now he felt stupid that he had yelled at her and then stomped off, but he wished she wouldn't always rub in the fact she could always do everything better than he could.

Just as Luke was reaching for his milk, the emergency siren went off again, the wail so loud it felt like it was inside his head. His hand jerked in midreach, knocking the glass over. He stood up, the chair falling over behind him.

"What's going on?" Theo asked.

Adam was in the room in seconds. "Luke, relax. Stay put until we know what's going on."

Luke took hold of the table, trying to breathe. Theo gave him a funny look and picked up the glass, even though the milk had already soaked through the tablecloth.

Isabelle came in. "System glitches, according to security ops. When the earthquake happened, some of the . . . uh . . . automatic sensors were thrown off, and the high winds are an issue." She looked at Theo like she had given away some big secret.

"How do they know for sure? They haven't had time to check everything out. They can't just assume it's all because of the earthquake," Luke said.

"They're not just assuming that," Adam said. "Everybody is doing their jobs step by step, running through checklists, but I'm sure everything is earthquake related."

"Sounds logical." Theo cut up more pancake. "Come on, Luke, Let's finish."

Luke tried to figure out which sensors were goofed up. The newest ones were part of a high-tech defense system, the IPDS, somewhere in the woods. He had overheard his dad talking to one of the agents about it. Once the system was triggered it sent out a special kind of ray that would cause extreme pain to anyone trying to get through the woods to the inner circle of build-ings. His dad thought it was too much, and they were safe enough with the Marines, but Luke liked the idea of something besides fences and soldiers keeping the bad guys out.

"Is it the inner perimeter defense system in the woods? The IPDS? Is something wrong with that?" Luke asked.

From the expression on Isabelle's face, Luke could tell she was surprised he knew about it.

Adam sighed. "We'll talk later about where you get your information, which, remember, may not be accurate. We're not going to talk about any-thing specific right now."

"It's probably not that, though," Luke said, try-ing to see if he would get a reaction. "I bet the earthquake would affect the buildings more. It's the lacing in some of the walls, isn't it? Some of the wires broke and the sensors detected it like someone is trying to break through."

Isabelle opened her mouth, but Adam spoke first. "Who knows? It could be anything. Did you tell Theo about the old secret door that used to be in one of the cabins?"

Luke knew Adam was trying to get him away from spilling any more security secrets. He wasn't supposed to know about the electric lacing either, but when he had seen some of the soldiers working inside Aspen, the presidential lodge, he figured it out. They had taken off part of the paneling and were checking a spiderweb of wiring underneath it, way more than the wiring needed for electrical outlets.

"A secret door?" Theo asked. "What was it used for?" He was looking around as if he expected to find it.

"Don't get too excited. It's not here anymore. The President who had it built was in a wheelchair. I can't remember his name." Luke looked at Adam.

"Franklin Delano Roosevelt," Adam said.

"Right. Anyway, he was really scared of fire, so they built a secret door in the wall of his bedroom he could open with a rope. I would have used it just to freak out the Secret Service. You know, sneak out and come around through the front door," Luke said, knowing this would get a rise out of Adam.

"Hilarious," Adam said, shaking his head. "Just a word of advice—don't ever climb out the window and try pulling a stunt like that."

"I know it wouldn't work. Some motion sensor would trigger as soon as I opened the window."

"Smart kid," Adam said. "I have good news. We're cleared to stay, and we're also cleared to go outside, as long as we stay in the inner zone."

"I think we should work on the robot in the tree house. Okay, Theo? It's really big and we can spread out."

"Nice," Theo said. "Can we take some doughnuts with us?"

"Sure, what kind?"

"How about the ones with chocolate frosting?"

Luke grabbed a huge napkin and piled doughnuts on it. "Come on. Let's go make the most amazing robot Camp David has ever seen."

12

The Main Gate

The SUV that pulled into the motel parking lot was just like the ones at the President's ranch, black, shiny, and spotless, as if specks of dust didn't dare land on it. The Secret Service agent driving it wore the typical dark suit and sunglasses, and Callie thought he must be roasting in the heat. She was roasting in her own jacket, but she was afraid to take it off in front of anyone, in case the kitten tried to get out. The man got out of the car and shook her father's hand.

"You must be Charlie Lansa. I'm Warren Erickson," he said. "We met last year in Colorado. I remember you make a mean enchilada."

That made Callie's dad smile.

"And you must be Callie." The man held out his hand to her.

Callie's right hand was still in her pocket around the kitten, trying to hold the pocket far enough open so the kitten could get some air but not be seen. She eased her hand out, hoping the cat wouldn't squeak. Little cat hairs stuck to her palm, which was all sweaty from the heat. She gave the agent's hand one shake, drawing her own hand back as quickly as she could.

"Let's get your luggage in," Agent Erickson said, opening up the back gate of the car. "It's about a twenty-minute ride."

Callie kept the backpack with her and climbed into the backseat, adjusting her jacket and the seat belt so it wouldn't press against the kitten, who was purring softly now.

As they were driving out of town, Callie's dad said, "Did you feel the earthquake? We were surprised."

"I just heard it was tremors spreading all the way from a big earthquake in Missouri," the agent said. "It's a major disaster there. As soon as we get back to Camp David, we'll be able to get more details."

Callie hoped their cabin didn't have a television. After anything horrible happened, it was scary to see it replayed over and over for days afterward.

Her dad spoke up, and Callie knew he was trying to change the subject away from the earthquake, so she wouldn't dwell on it. "Looks like this area hasn't seen rain in months."

"We've hardly seen a drop of rain all summer." The agent turned up the air conditioner. Callie wasn't surprised the talk had turned to weather, though she never understood why adults spent so much time jabbering about it. "I'm afraid we're going to lose some trees. It's way too dry. Have you ever been to Camp David, Chef Lansa?"

"No, I've never been there, so this will be a real treat, right, Callie?"

"Right," Callie said, knowing the expected answer.

"There's a lot of history there. President Roosevelt used the camp first, and he called it Shangri La. President Eisenhower changed the name to Camp David in the 1950s. He named it for his grandson. Supposedly, any president can change the name if they want, but no one has since then."

Great. Any day now, Callie thought, the newspapers would announce Camp David had been renamed Camp Luke.

Agent Erickson gave a huge sneeze. "Excuse me," he said. He sneezed again. "Callie, I know you have been on the ranch when the President is there, but I'd like to go over the rules again."

"I know the rules," Callie said. "If a Secret Service agent tells me not to do something, I'm supposed to listen and obey, just like at the ranch."

"Callie," her dad said, "you need to listen now."

"We'll arrange a tour later," the agent continued, "but there's a staff pool, and even a bowling alley. It's easy to find everything. Most of the buildings are clustered together, either on the main road, or right off it on the smaller access drives. Any building with a guard in front of it is obviously off-limits."

Callie wanted to say, "Duh," but she knew her dad would get mad. Agent Erickson must think she had the brains of a five-year-old.

"Guests at Camp David can use the woodland trails inside the fence at certain times. If you are on the trails, you don't want to wander off into the woods." Agent Erickson looked back over his shoulder, probably to see if she was paying attention. "Believe me, you don't want to startle a Marine guard in the woods. I understand you're friends with Luke Brockett."

"Um, sort of." The kitten was licking her finger again and Callie tried not to laugh.

"Of course, Luke knows all the rules. He'll know where you can and can't go." Warren sneezed three times in a row.

"Excuse me again," he said.

"Sounds like allergies," Callie's dad said.

"Shouldn't be allergies. I'm not allergic to anything but cats."

"I picked up a cat outside the motel," Callie said quickly. "Maybe some of its fur got on my clothes."

Warren sniffed. "That's probably it. I just can't stand cats."

The kitten gave a tiny meow, so Callie pretended to cough. She pulled her camera out of her backpack. There wasn't much to see, but at least the clicking of the shutter might cover any sounds from the kitten.

The agent frowned in the rearview mirror.

"That camera will have to stay in your cabin," he said. "You can't take photos at Camp David."

"What if I show you all the pictures I take before I leave?" Callie asked. Now that the camera was in her hands, she knew she couldn't put it away for a week. It went with her everywhere, because she never knew when a good shot would appear. "You can delete all the ones you want. I won't take any pictures of buildings."

"Well, maybe," he said. "Even if we get permission, though, you can't take even one picture of Luke Brockett. That is absolutely against the rules."

"No problem." She didn't want to take pictures of Luke! "Could I take a few pictures before we get there? Out of the window, I mean. My aunt Kate wanted me to e-mail her lots of pictures."

"That's fine, but we will be in the restricted area in just a minute."

The SUV turned onto a road marked with a sign: CATOCTIN MOUNTAIN PARK. Callie snapped pictures of everything, even if nothing seemed very interesting. They passed two people dressed for hiking.

Agent Erickson motioned at the hikers and slowed the car as the road narrowed. "Camp

David is located in a national park, so even outside the fence we are surrounded by woods."

A black shape appeared in the camera's viewfinder. Callie tried to make out what it was. It was moving, but not as fast as the car. She held down the zoom button.

"It's a bear! I see a bear!" she yelled.

"Where?" Agent Erickson braked as if afraid the bear was in front of the car.

"There, over there, in the forest." The bear was moving fast, his big body swaying from side to side. "He's gone," Callie said, lowering the camera and turning off the shutter. "Wow! I can't see it anymore. That was great."

"You were lucky," Agent Erickson said. "There aren't that many in this part of Maryland." The car moved forward again.

Callie shifted around, trying to put the camera away and take off her jacket without hurting the kitten. She positioned the pocket and the kitten in her lap. When she leaned over to peek in, her braid dangled down and the kitten stuck a paw out to bat at it.

Agent Erickson sneezed again. Startled, Callie hid the kitten's paw.

The road became steeper until they came to a

wooden fence covered with vines. Two security cameras were mounted on either side of a big wooden gate.

"It's just like the ranch," Callie said. "I bet the electric fence is inside this one."

"You're right. This fence is meant to blend in with the surroundings and warn off anybody who might get this close. I'm glad you're old enough to know to stay away from the electric fence. When the President is in residence we don't turn off the fence, and that's why we usually don't let staff children up here."

The wooden gate opened and Agent Erickson drove the car through, stopping before a much more imposing metal gate. On either side of it were thick chain-link sections held in place by concrete pillars. A guard with a dog came forward. Callie saw another guard watching them from a gatehouse inside the fence. The gatehouse looked more like the visitor center in the state park than a top-security checkpoint.

"Morning, Agent Erickson." The guard peered at them through the window. "You must be Charlie and Callie Lansa."

The dog kept sniffing around the car, looking for bombs. The same thing happened at the ranch every time a car came to the gatehouse when the President was there. The kitten gave a faint squeak and the dog looked up, alert, his ears pointed forward.

"Is that a German shepherd? What's its name?" Callie asked loudly, trying to drown out the kitten. She already knew it wasn't a shepherd, because the agents at the ranch used the same breed as this one. Her dad looked at her strangely.

"He's a Belgian Malinois named Vulcan," the guard said. Luckily the dog was well trained. He knew she had the kitten, but since finding cats wasn't his job, he moved on.

Callie prayed he, if the kitten was a he, would stay quiet long enough to get to the cabin. Once they were inside Camp David, it was hard to imagine anyone would kick a kitten out. She knew Luke had a dog, even though Comet had never been brought to the ranch. He was always on the First Family's holiday cards trying to look cute, and he even had his own page on the White House website. What kind of dog needed his own web page?

"Callie, are you listening to me?" her dad said.

"What?"

"Once we put our stuff down, I want to go

shopping with the agent on duty to see what's available. You'll be okay for a bit?"

Callie knew her dad was talking about the same routine they followed at the ranch. The Secret Service agents accompanied a staff person who did the grocery shopping, never going to the same store twice in a row, to keep the President's food safe from tampering.

"Sure, Dad, I'll be fine." Callie was relieved. With her dad gone, it would be easier to find a spot to hide the kitten, until she could find a good time to ask to keep him.

The sniffer dog barked. Startled, Callie huddled down in the seat.

"Is there a problem?" Agent Erickson asked.

"No, I don't know what's gotten into the dog," the guard said. "He's been acting jumpy all morning. Guess it was the earthquake, but I'm surprised he's still worked up. You're all clear."

13

The Center

"Sal, what's the decision about Luke?" President Brockett asked as he caught sight of the agent talking to George Michelson, the head of his security detail.

"We've decided Luke is better off here, sir," Sal said. "There's been minor damage all over to roads and bridges, and reports of fires in Washington from broken gas lines, so until we know the extent of the problems, we'll stick with our original plan."

"Fine." A blast of wind muffled the President's response. He straightened his tie and smoothed his hair. "George, how soon can I leave?"

14

The Tree House

CAMP DAVID

When Luke and Theo got back to their room, it took only a few minutes to collect what they needed. "If you bring the suitcase with the parts, I'll carry my laptop and the food," Luke said. He took his pocketknife off the table by the bed and slipped it in his pocket. He wasn't allowed to have it at the White House, but he liked carrying it around at Camp David, even though so far he'd only used it to cut up fruit.

"Is your laptop charged? You don't have electricity in the tree house, do you?" Theo asked.

"No," Luke said. "I want to run a big extension

cord so I can put in some lights, but that idea hasn't gone anywhere yet. The laptop has enough charge for an hour or so. That should be enough time to work out the program for the robot. Once we download it, the robot has plenty of its own battery power."

"What are we going to get the robot to grab?" Theo asked.

"The kit came with some plastic balls. We can just use those. And I was thinking about your idea of the sound sensor. I have a whistle we can use with it." Luke rummaged around in the drawer of his nightstand. "Someday I'm going to use it to train Comet to do tricks."

Hearing his name, Comet crawled out from under the bed and put his head on Luke's foot.

"Are you coming too?" Luke said, scratching the spot behind Comet's ear that made the dog's back foot thump. "Are you done acting like a scaredy-cat?" Comet sat up and barked once, thumping his tail.

"Do the agents have to come up in the tree house too?" Theo asked. "That would feel weird."

"No, they'll just stay close enough to see us."

"Okay," Theo said. He had gone back to his notebook, checking off items on a list. "I think we have what we need." He pulled out his pocket watch and wrote down the time. Theo checked the watch constantly. Luke had given up teasing him about it. Theo's uncle had given it to him, claiming it once belonged to Orville Wright, who used it to time one of Wilbur's early flights. Luke wasn't sure he believed that, but Theo did.

"Let's go. Come on, boy." Comet barked again and then followed after them out the door. In the hall Luke said to Adam, "We're ready."

"Speeder is on his way to the tree house." Isabelle spoke into the microphone attached to her wrist.

"Speeder?" Theo said to Luke.

"Speeder is me," Luke explained, embarrassed. "Everybody has a code name, and they gave me that when I was a little kid. Adam, can't we change it?"

"Maybe," Adam said. "I'll have to talk to Sal. Maybe we could change it to 'Monkey,' since you're always climbing trees. Or maybe we could change it to 'Drummer,' since you drive everyone crazy with your drumming."

"You're just jealous you can't do it," Luke said. "Listen to this." He beat out a complicated pattern on the wall.

"You're right, I can't do that," Adam said. "You beat me in drumming talent."

"Who's on duty after you?" Luke asked. "We want to roast marshmallows tonight."

"Brian and the new guy, Grant, were supposed to be on duty." Adam grinned. "Don't tease Brian about this when he gets back, but the earthquake made a lamp fall over in his room, and Brian tripped on it getting out of bed. He's down in Hagerstown getting an X-ray. He may have broken his wrist."

"He won't be happy about that," Luke said.

"No, he won't," Adam agreed. "I don't know who'll be teaming up with Grant yet. I don't know about the marshmallows either. The fire danger is so high we aren't supposed to have any open flames."

"You told me the chefs here can make anything," Theo said. "Do you think we could do ice-cream sundaes?"

Here was a reason Theo would definitely want to come back. "Sure," Luke said. "They have all sorts of toppings and flavors, just like a real ice-cream place." Luke remembered going to an ice-cream place one time, and even with all the photographers taking his picture, it had been great.

"Nice."

Outside, gusts of wind made the heat worse, like hot furnace blasts of air.

Theo whistled when he saw the tree house. "That's big. How many kids can fit in there?"

"I don't know. I'm the only one who has ever been up in it, besides the agents and the crew who built it." Theo was the first person Luke had ever had to visit.

"Boy, my dad told me about a tree house he had when he was a kid that sounded fantastic, but I don't think it topped this one," Theo said. "I should have worked harder on him to help me build one."

"My dad helped me," Luke said. That wasn't exactly a lie. Pierce Brockett had come out to check on the progress while Luke and the Navy staff on the building and repair team were working on it.

"The best part of it is the pulley system. We can raise and lower a crate," Luke said. That part of the tree house was his dad's major contribution, at least the idea of it.

"Every tree house should have a block-and-tackle system," his dad had said. "It was one of Archimedes' most important inventions."

Luke didn't care who invented it, but he liked putting it together and trying to figure out the right arrangement of pulleys and ropes. When they first put it up, he wanted to get in the crate himself and have someone hoist him up, but everyone nixed that idea as too dangerous.

Theo started to climb up the ladder with the suitcase.

"Wait," Luke said. "We can put everything in the crate and pull it up."

"I could just carry stuff up."

"No, the whole point of the pulley system is to make it easier."

Luke climbed up, leaving Theo to put stuff in the crate. When Theo gave him a signal to go, Luke pulled on a rope and hoisted the crate up. He loved working the ropes because he could pretend he was on a sailing ship, pulling up the sails.

The crate came level with Luke and he looped the rope around the hook they had installed just for that purpose. Once he had unloaded the crate, he lowered it back down.

"Comet, your turn," Luke called, pointing at the crate. Comet got up slowly and walked over. The wind was making the crate sway.

"In, boy," Luke ordered. Comet looked up at Luke apologetically, then lay down, deciding to stay put.

Theo climbed up. "Let's lay everything out in a row first."

"Why don't I build while you work on the programming?" Luke said as he opened the suitcase. He didn't want to spend the time sorting out everything.

"That's a good idea. I figured out the steps already. We need to program it to move forward, then stop, then grab, then return to base, all on sound commands."

Luke turned his laptop on. Once the robot program was open, Luke ran through the menu options with Theo.

"This is great!" Theo said. "We'll be able to make it do all sorts of things." He sat down with the laptop on his knees and his notebook open beside him.

Luke had most of the robot together in ten minutes. "How's it going?" he asked Theo.

"I need to think for a minute." Theo got up and paced three steps one way and then three steps the other. When Theo said he had to think, he always paced exactly three steps, no matter how much room he had.

"I think our next robot after this one should be a squirrel robot," Luke said, looking out over the trees, tapping on the window ledge, already bored with Theo's thinking. The tree house windows didn't have glass in them, but they had shutters that could be closed in case of rain.

"Wouldn't that be great?" Luke eyed the nearest tree. "It could have stealthlike spy capabilities. Nobody pays attention to squirrels. I've been watching them, and it's incredible how they can jump between thin branches. They jump and then hold on while the branch sways up and down."

Theo stopped pacing. "How would you get a squirrel robot's extensors to clasp onto a branch at the right moment? Even if we could program a remote control, your reflexes wouldn't be quick enough to operate it."

"Maybe we could put a lot of extensors on the front of it, already partway closed," Luke said. "Some would catch on, don't you think? If I jumped like a squirrel with my hands already closed, I bet it would be easy to catch. I'll show you."

"That sounds like a terrible idea," Theo said.

"No, it will work." Luke looked out the front

window. Isabelle was standing in the shade, angled so she could see the tree house and the road. Adam was talking to Sal by the road.

Luke went to the back of the tree house and swung a leg over the windowsill. There was a maple tree with a branch almost close enough to reach.

"It's a really terrible idea," Theo said.

"No, watch."

Luke climbed up on the edge of the window, crouching down, using one hand for balance until he was stable. He pushed off, both hands in front of him, fingers curled. The second he was in the air was just like flying, but the great feeling was all too short. He caught the branch of the maple tree, surprised at how much it hurt when his hands hit the rough bark. The branch bent down, then up again, and then down, making a loud crack as it split from the trunk and plummeted to the ground, taking Luke with it.

15

Air and Ground

Still holding on to the branch, Luke fell, hitting feetfirst. One end of the branch drove into the ground and Luke pushed away from it, toppling over. He lay looking up at the sky.

Adam and Isabelle were there in seconds. Comet leaned over him, whimpering.

"It's okay, boy," Luke said, getting up, trying not to wince when he felt pain shoot through his knee. He put his hands behind him so no one could see the scrapes.

"What are you doing?" Isabelle asked, her voice sharp. "You could have broken your neck!"

Theo climbed down. "I won't say I told you so."

"Experimenting with gravity again, I see." Luke's dad came around the tree, followed by two of his agents. Christine trailed behind them, checking her watch.

Adam and Isabelle stood up straight, and Isabelle's eyes went wide. "I'm sorry, Mr. President," she said. "We didn't see him climb out the back." Isabelle stuttered a little, and Adam's face turned bright red. Luke realized they could be in trouble for his bad idea.

"It's not your fault." Pierce Brockett examined the broken branch. "I know this boy can surprise you. Someday he will learn, I hope."

"I was . . . was just trying to see how squirrels jump from branch to branch," Luke said. As soon as the words were out of his mouth, he knew how stupid he sounded.

"Hmmm, we'll talk another time about 'look before you leap,' though I never expected you to be actually leaping." Luke's dad smiled a little, but he didn't look happy.

Luke put his head down and scuffed the ground. The dry leaves flew up and some dirt got on his dad's perfectly shined shoes.

"I'm not sure I should leave you here," Pierce Brockett said. "Maybe you and Theo should go back to Washington after all."

"Please, Dad. I promise I won't do anything like that again. We have all sorts of stuff planned. We want to try the robot over rough ground and see how it does. We can't do that at the White House." Luke knew he sounded like he was begging, but he was desperate. He didn't want to leave now.

"Everything okay?" Sal asked, walking over to his dad.

While the two men decided his and Theo's fate, the helicopters started up in the camp's airfield. Everywhere his dad went there were helicopters ready for him. Even when he traveled on Air Force One, another cargo plane carrying helicopters went along too. Normally Luke loved riding in them, but not today.

"All right. You and Theo can stay," Luke's dad said. "I talked to your mother and she will be calling you in a few minutes. I'm counting on you to stay out of trouble. Theo, I know you have a good head on your shoulders." He said nothing about Luke's head.

"We'll be careful, sir," Theo replied.

"It's time, Mr. President," Christine said.

Luke watched his father's face turn serious.

"I have to get going," Luke's dad said. "I expect to hear an astonishing report about the robot's capabilities. I'll try to call tonight."

"Okay."

The chief of staff walked up, holding out a cell phone. "More damage updates, sir."

As his dad took the phone and turned to go, Luke said, "I'm . . . I'm sorry about all those people out in Missouri."

Pierce Brockett came back and put his hand on Luke's shoulder. "I know," he said in a soft voice only Luke could hear. "But what do we always say? You didn't ask to be the President's son, and the weight of the country isn't on your shoulders. I'm glad you are here having fun. It's something I can think about when I need a break. Good luck with the robot."

"Thanks, Dad."

"Sir, the helicopters are ready to go," one of his dad's agents said.

"Let's get a move on. *Dimidium facti qui coepit habet*." President Brockett strode off toward the landing pad. Luke couldn't remember what this one meant. His dad had too many sayings. The only one he knew for sure was *festina lente*— "make haste slowly." His dad said it to him all the time because he thought Luke was too impulsive.

"'He who has begun has the work half done,'" Theo murmured as he came up.

"What?"

"Your dad just said, 'He who has begun has the work half done.' Horace said it first."

"Oh, right."

"Excuse me, Luke," Sal said. "Your mother is on the phone for you." He held out a cell phone and then went over to Adam and Isabelle. Luke hoped Sal wouldn't chew them out for his stupid trick.

"Hi, Mom. How was the wedding?" Luke's mom was in England for the wedding of somebody royal.

"It hasn't happened yet." Her voice sounded as if she were around the corner. "I have to leave for the church in just a minute. Luke, don't forget Callie is coming with her dad today. I want you to be nice to her. Chef Lansa told me Callie isn't excited about moving to Washington."

Luke could hear people talking in the background.

"I have to go," his mother said. "I'll see you in two days. Have fun. Love you." The phone clicked off.

The sound from the helicopters grew louder. In a few seconds, they rose over the trees, turning to the south. There were always three identical helicopters in the air whenever his dad flew, so no one could tell for sure which one held the President. Anyone trying to shoot a missile at the helicopter wouldn't know which one to target. Luke watched until they were specks in the distance.

"Look at the fog," Theo said. "That's very strange." He pointed to the east, where a clump of fog hung over the forest outside of Camp David, down in the valley where the campgrounds and hiking trails were located. "I thought it was too dry for fog."

Sal looked surprised. "That's not fog; that's smoke, and that means fire." He held out his hand for his cell phone. "Why can't these campers obey the rules? I'll make sure the park district knows."

Luke watched the smoke for a moment. He couldn't see any actual fire, and the smoke was a long way away, at least a mile or so.

Theo went back to the ladder and called, "Let's get the robot finished so we can try it out."

"Okay." Luke followed him up. At the top he

looked out at the smoke and then at Sal, still talking on his phone. When Sal wanted something done, it happened, so that fire would be out in no time.

16

Hemlock Cabin

After the guard with the dog cleared them past the gate, Callie relaxed. The road continued through more woods, and then the woods disappeared and something like a fancy resort came into view. Callie couldn't believe it. It wasn't like a camp at all; everything was landscaped and manicured to perfection. The flowers in front of the big stone-and-wood buildings looked like they didn't dare turn brown or lose a petal, and the sidewalks were spotless. Guards with guns stood statuelike in front of most of the buildings. Callie couldn't imagine a more boring job.

"This is the staff area," Agent Erickson said as he turned off the main road onto a long drive and pulled up in front of a small wooden cabin. "Why don't you drop your bags off, and I'll take you up to the kitchen." He turned off the car and pulled out a key card.

"Sounds good," Callie's dad said.

Agent Erickson took their bags out of the back. "Your cabin is called Hemlock. Most of the buildings are named after plants. The main kitchen is in Laurel Lodge, the conference building. Callie, if it's okay with your dad, you should come along so you can start to get a feel for the place."

"Good idea," her dad said. "We can just put the bags inside the front door."

As soon as her dad unlocked the door, Callie went around him into the cabin. "I want to see where I'm going to sleep," she said.

"We can't keep Agent Erickson waiting."

"I won't. Can I have this room?" Callie opened the door to a room decorated in brown and green, with two twin beds.

"Yes, but come on. We're just dropping off the bags."

"Let me get rid of my jacket," Callie said. She put it on the bed, and while the kitten wriggled out of the pocket, Callie hurried to get her dad out of the cabin.

When they got back in the car, Callie saw three helicopters in the distance. "What's happening?" she asked.

"The President is going back to the White House and then to Missouri to oversee the earth-quake situation. For right now you're to stay put," Agent Erickson said.

Laurel Lodge was as big as any hotel Callie had ever seen. A small waterfall spilled out in front, falling into a pool of orange and white fish swim-ming lazily in circles.

"I'll take you in the front entrance," Agent Erickson said. "But there is a back door." Mean-ing, Callie thought, *Next time, don't come in the front; you are just the staff.*

They went through an entrance hall full of paint-ings like a museum, and then through a door at the end of the back hallway into the kitchen. Callie and her dad were introduced to the Navy chef, Owen, and soon the two chefs were talking away. Callie knew she had to make her escape before Chef Owen could start on some incredibly detailed tour showing off every possible spoon and pan.

"Dad, I'd like to go back to the cabin, but I'm really thirsty. Can I take a big glass of milk to the cabin?"

"This isn't like the ranch, Callie," her dad answered. "You can't just take food from the kitchen. I'll buy some things this morning for our cabin."

"I think we can let her have a glass of milk," Chef Owen said. "Are you hungry too, young lady?"

"No, sir," Callie said. "Just thirsty."

When Chef Owen opened one of the refrigerators, Callie didn't feel bad about asking for milk. It held at least ten cartons, both white and chocolate. Chef Owen handed her the glass and she sipped it.

"Thank you," she said. "Can I go now, Dad?"

"Sure, go ahead. Here, take my key until we can get another one. Can you find your way?"

"Yes, Dad." Callie rolled her eyes at him, but he was already examining the espresso maker.

Callie walked back to the cabin as fast as she could without spilling the milk. When she came into her room, the kitten was wobbling around on the bed, mewing softly.

"Come here, little fellow," Callie said, picking him up. "You're going to like this." The cabin had its own small kitchen, and Callie found a saucer. When she put the kitten and the saucer on the floor, the poor thing was so hungry he put his front paws right in the milk, trying to get at it. He wasn't very good at lapping. He kept sticking his whole nose down in the milk, and then every few seconds he would come up for air and sneeze.

"I'm going to name you Tocho," Callie said, sitting on the floor beside him. The kitten was so cute trying to drink the milk, Callie knew she had to take his picture. Nobody could get mad at her for taking pictures inside the cabin. There was nothing special about the place at all.

The kitten didn't even look at her while she snapped away. It was funny to see the little droplets of milk all around his mouth and on his whiskers. He was a mess, and so hungry. Callie filled the saucer again.

"Milk should hold you for now," she said. "At lunch I'll get you more food." There was one problem, she realized. There was no litter box. She couldn't leave the kitten go to the bathroom on the floor of the cabin. She would have to take him outside.

Maybe Luke would help her convince people to let her keep the kitten. Maybe he had forgotten about falling off Hania. She wished he would go back to being the old Luke. They used to spend every summer running around the ranch, exploring all the different rock outcroppings, looking for gold and silver. The first time they found some galena, they were sure they had discovered silver and were going to be rich. Maybe if she gave him the galena she had brought with her, it would remind him of the fun they had and they could go back to being friends again.

The front door opened. "Callie, I'm leaving soon," her dad called.

She pushed the saucer under the bed with her foot, scooping up the kitten with her other hand, stuffing him back in the jacket pocket. He was so sleepy, he didn't even open his eyes. She picked up her jacket just as her father came by.

"Why are you bringing that? It's hot as blazes outside."

"I just feel cold today," Callie said, easing the jacket on carefully. She felt the sweat start to trickle down her back. As soon as her dad left she would find someplace to put Tocho down outside.

"I hope you aren't getting sick."

"No, I'm fine." She smiled brightly.

"I hope so. Agent Erickson told me Luke is probably in his tree house. It's behind the President's lodge, the big building called Aspen, past the swimming pool. Come on, I'll show you the way."

Her dad was already out in the hall, so she grabbed her camera too, put it around her neck, and shifted it so it was under her jacket at her side. She'd take pictures only when no one was looking. Agent Erickson had probably forgotten anyway.

As they walked up the road, Callie's dad told her all about the size of the kitchen staff and the appliances. She could tell he was happy, so she didn't make any sarcastic remarks, even when he got excited about the number of dishwashers in the place.

Partway down the road, the SUV pulled up again, or maybe it was another one, because there was a different agent behind the wheel. "Are you ready, Chef Lansa?" the man asked.

"Do you mind, Callie?" Her dad pointed to the top of a big tree behind a building. "There's the tree house, or at least a corner of it."

"Go ahead, Dad. I'll be fine." She would say hi to Luke and see what he was like now. She was willing to put up with a lot if he would help convince people she could keep Tocho.

17

The Inner Zone

The tree house wasn't the flat little platform she was expecting. She should have realized Luke wouldn't have anything ordinary. This probably even had running water and electricity. Luke and a tall boy stood at the base of the tree, talking and looking at a notebook. Luke's dog sat by his side. As she drew closer, Callie heard Luke say, "She doesn't know anything about robots. When we want to work on it, we'll just tell her we have a summer assignment for school. She's really bossy and she usually doesn't listen, but that should get rid of her. She only likes horses anyway. I think robots are too complicated for her. They don't have hooves." He laughed.

"Too complicated?" Callie yelled as she came up and grabbed his arm, pulling him around. "You think I'm stupid just because I don't care about your little bits of plastic? At least I'm not a baby who can't even take falling off a horse." There was no way she was going to give him the galena now.

Before she could push him down, Luke's dog jumped at her, barking, and a Secret Service agent, a woman, was there between them.

"Let's just calm down now," the woman said. "What's going on here?"

"Nothing, Isabelle." Luke backed away from Callie. "We were just goofing around."

Another agent walked up to them. "Everything okay, Luke?"

"Everything's fine," Luke said.

"You must be Callie Lansa. I'm Adam."

Callie looked up to see a man with dark hair and nice green eyes and a face that looked like it smiled once in a while.

"Hi," she mumbled.

"We're glad you made it here. It sounds like you three will have a terrific week." The man grinned at all of them like nothing had happened. He had a nice voice, Callie thought, like someone who didn't just bark orders all the time.

Everybody was silent, and then the tall boy said, "I'm Theo."

"Oh, yeah, this is my friend Theo," Luke said, not even looking at her.

"Well, now that you're all here, I can give my little speech," Adam said. "I'm sure Agent Erickson already told you about how things work, Callie, but there are a few more things everyone needs to hear. Luke, Theo, are you listening? Everybody needs to stay out of the woods today. Callie, some of the security systems are being checked because of the earthquake, and they're doing testing by sections."

"How long is it going to take?" Luke said.

"I don't know, but don't plan on any hikes until we get the all-clear. How's the robot coming?"

"It's going to be amazing!" Luke said. "We were just going to test it out." He put the robot down on the ground. "Theo, why don't you put the ball about ten feet away?"

Callie could tell Luke had forgotten about her. He was rocking forward and backward drumming on his legs, totally focused on the robot.

When Theo had the ball in place Luke turned

the robot on. "Theo, do you want to do the whistle?"

Luke pulled the whistle out of his pocket and handed it to Theo. When Theo blew on it, the robot moved forward, making a pinging noise.

"We programmed it to ping like a sonar signal while it's moving toward something. Isn't that great?" Luke said. "Once it grabs the ball and comes back to the starting point, it's programmed to play a fanfare."

The dog crept toward the robot, growling, and Callie felt the kitten shift in her pocket. As the robot drew within inches of the ball, Theo blew the whistle two more times. The robot stopped and closed its claws on the ball, but when they clamped on, the ball popped out over the top of them.

"The ball is too slippery," Theo said. "And the claws are squeezing too tightly."

Callie moved over to it so she could get a closer look. "Why don't you just stick something spongy to the claws? It could hold on to things better that way."

"Good idea," Theo said. "We can fasten some pieces of foam to each of the extensors. What do you think, Luke?"

"I don't think it will work," Luke said. "We just need to adjust the rotation of the gear to the claws."

"Callie's idea is worth a try, at least," Theo said. "That way the robot could hold on to things of different sizes."

The kitten shifted again and Comet started sniffing at Callie's boot.

She tried to use her foot to push him away, but he didn't back up. The dog moved his nose from her boot to her leg and growled at her. She put her hand in her pocket, holding on to Tocho so he wouldn't poke his head out.

"Weird," Luke said. "Comet likes everybody. Maybe you smell funny."

"Thanks a lot."

"No, I meant . . . I meant maybe you smell like your dog or something."

Comet came closer, almost sticking his nose in her pocket. The kitten squirmed and hissed, and then gave a loud enough meow for everyone to hear.

"What's that?" Luke asked, just as Comet gave one startled bark.

"It sounded like a cat," Theo said.

For a moment Callie wondered if she could

bluff her way out of it and claim she was just clearing her throat or something, but Tocho stuck his head out of her pocket before she could do anything. Comet barked again, bringing his face close to Callie's pocket, growling.

"Luke, get your dog away. He's scaring my kitten." Callie put her hand on Tocho in case Comet jumped at them.

"You brought a kitten into Camp David?" Theo asked, as Luke grabbed hold of Comet's collar. "Is that allowed?"

Everybody looked at Adam.

"I don't think it ever occurred to anyone to make a rule," Adam said. "The people who visit here don't normally carry their pets around in their pockets. Now that it's been done, though, someone will have to make a rule against it."

"You won't take him away from me, will you?" Callie asked, worried. She took Tocho out of her pocket and held him close, glancing at Adam. Adam didn't look like he was angry, but she knew from past experience that it was hard to know what Secret Service agents were thinking. The kitten stopped struggling and snuggled closer.

"We'll see," Adam said.

"He's so little, he won't hurt anything, I promise.

His name is Tocho. It means 'panther' in Hopi," she said, not knowing what else to say.

Luke cracked up laughing. "That little smudge of fur doesn't look much like a panther."

"He will when he's bigger," Callie said defensively. "At least he's going to grow into something. Your dog is already grown and still looks like a stuffed animal."

"So what!" Luke yelled. At the sound of Luke's raised voice, Comet started barking.

Tocho struggled in Callie's hands. He was so skinny, he squeezed through her grip and jumped to the ground. Arching his back, Tocho spit at Comet. The dog broke away from Luke and skidded to a stop inches from the kitten. He sniffed at Tocho cautiously and wagged his tail, but then the kitten lost his nerve and took off at a zigzag run over the grass and into the woods. Comet hesitated just for a moment and then dashed after him. Within seconds, the dog caught up. Just as Comet's jaws were about to close on the kitten, Tocho turned abruptly to one side. Comet lost his balance, tumbling over. The little kitten kept running.

"Stop, boy!" Luke yelled. Comet picked himself up and took off again after the kitten.

"He'll hurt Tocho if he catches him!" Callie yelled. She ran after Comet, not able to see Tocho anymore. "Get your stupid dog, Luke!"

She could hear Luke behind her, and then Adam roared, "Luke, stop *now*! Don't go in the woods! It's too dangerous! Callie!" She looked back. Luke had stopped and Adam and the woman were running toward them. What was in there? Callie slowed and then came to a halt. Neither animal was in sight now. The agents and Luke jogged up to her, Theo coming behind.

"Don't go in the woods," Adam repeated, his voice totally unlike the friendly one she had heard just a few minutes ago. He didn't even look the same. She could see the tension in his body, like he was ready to leap at something.

"Adam, what's going to happen to Comet?" Luke sounded panicked. "Is the defense system on? It could kill Comet, couldn't it?"

"Calm down, Luke," Adam said. "I'll notify the camp commander and have them stop the testing until we can get Comet. They may not even be testing that section of the woods right now." Adam moved away.

"What kind of defense system do you have here that will kill animals?" Callie asked. "There's nothing like that at the ranch."

"It's new. These boxes are mounted on the trees and they send out this radiation, kind of like microwave rays, and they cause so much pain you think you're on fire before you pass out." Luke was talking so fast his words were tumbling over one another. "I overheard my dad say that it killed some goats when they tested the prototype. Why did you bring a cat here anyway?" Luke's voice rose to a yell. "Comet could get hurt!"

18

Trapped

Luke could feel his insides twisting up, and in his fury he wanted to hit someone. He tried to get around Isabelle, but the agent grabbed him.

"*Luke!* Get control of yourself!" she ordered.

"How far away is it?" Through his rage Luke heard the worry in Adam's voice and saw he was on his cell phone. Behind him, Luke could see that people were pouring out of the buildings. A group of Marines started jogging up the main road.

"What's going on, Adam?" Isabelle asked.

Adam snapped his phone shut. "The forest fire east of here Sal called in is spreading. Just as a precaution, we are all going to go back to

Washington. The camp will be shut down until the fire is under control. There's an evacuation plan we have practiced, so let's just follow the procedure. Sal is meeting us in front of Aspen."

"Adam, what about Comet!" Luke tried to keep his voice down. "Were they testing that section?"

"Comet will be fine," Adam said. "The testing has halted so we can evacuate. I'm sure the fire won't spread this far, and we'll send someone back for Comet as soon as we can."

"I think I smell the fire," Callie said suddenly. "How close is it?" She wrapped her arms around herself.

"If you can smell it, it's probably not too far away," Theo said. "I think I can smell it too."

Callie gave a strangled whisper: "I don't like fire."

"Isabelle, call for another agent to join us ASAP," Adam said. "Luke, you can stand at the edge of the woods and call for Comet. He'll come back. We have a few minutes before the cars are ready. As soon as another agent gets here, I'm going to go talk to Sal and work out some details. Let's do this one step at a time, but you have to promise not to go into the woods." Adam moved closer as if afraid Luke would bolt.

"I'm not leaving without Comet." Luke walked toward the forest and stopped just on the edge. Both agents followed a step behind.

"He'll come back. Why don't you two help Luke call for him?" Adam said to Theo and Callie.

"Comet!" Luke screamed. "Comet!" He wished he had trained Comet better. He meant to, but he had never gotten around to it. He thought about making a run for the woods, except he knew there was no way he could get in without one of the agents tackling him.

"Comet!" Theo and Callie both yelled together. "Tocho!" Callie called.

Everyone waited, and Luke strained to see any bit of white amid the trees. There was nothing.

"Luke." Sal came up, startling Luke so much he jumped and bumped into Sal's arm. "Luke, we have to go."

"What's going to happen to Comet?" Luke said, watching Sal's eyes. Sal wouldn't lie to him.

Sal hesitated a moment. "I don't know, but dogs are smart, and they're good at taking care of themselves. Now, we've talked many times about emergencies. You know what your father would expect you to do."

Luke's throat closed up and he felt tears in his

eyes. "Yes," he said. "Let's go."

"What about me?" Callie asked. "Where's my dad?" Luke was surprised to hear how small her voice sounded.

"You are coming with us, miss," Sal said. "The agent with your father has already been notified and they're all on their way to Washington. Theo, I have someone calling your family. They'll know you're on your way back too." Sal spoke into his microphone: "Speeder is on his way."

Luke followed Sal, turning around every few steps in case Comet came out of the woods. He couldn't see anything moving in the underbrush, but birds kept flying up out of the trees and then over their heads and away. When they reached the parking lot by Aspen Lodge, another of Luke's agents, Grant, stood near the three SUVs.

"We left the robot by the tree house," Theo said.

"My laptop is up in it," Luke said.

"Tocho is still—" Callie said.

"We need to go *now*," Sal interrupted, pointing to the cars. "The first rule of an evacuation is not to take time to get things. I'm sure they'll have the fire under control before it even gets close, so your things will be fine. We'll have someone collect them when the camp opens back up."

"I see smoke." They all looked as Callie pointed. Gray puffy smoke rose up in the east. It was so thick no one could mistake it for fog now.

"Luke, you will be in the middle car with your friends," Sal said. "Adam, you drive Luke. Grant will go with you. Isabelle, you take the trail car."

Sal's phone rang. They all waited while he listened. Luke saw the kitchen staff drive by in two white vans. A military truck full of Marines followed them.

"Let's go," Sal said, motioning them to the middle car. He waited until they were inside and then he got in the lead car.

When they were all seated, Grant said, "Buckle up, everyone." He leaned over the back and watched them fasten their seat belts. As the SUVs pulled out of the parking lot and onto the road, another truck full of Marines slowed to let them in front.

"Is everybody leaving?" Luke asked. He couldn't imagine Camp David empty. "Even the command center staff?"

"Everybody," Adam said. "It's just a precaution because of the dry conditions and the wind. Don't worry."

"What about the fire trucks here? Why can't they just go put out the fire?" Luke asked.

"They're already headed to it, but there's no ready supply of water, besides what's in the pumper truck. I'm sure they will get it under control, though."

"Are you sure?" Callie asked. "Wildfires in California get out of control all the time."

"It's not the same here," Theo said. "The vegetation is totally different, and that affects the speed of a fire. Of course, the winds and all the dead plants aren't going to help."

"Great," Callie said.

"Callie, did your dad know you had the kitten?" Adam asked from the front seat.

"No!" The last thing she wanted was for her dad to get in trouble. "I just had him in my pocket the whole time. My dad told me to give it to the lady at the hotel. He didn't know anything about it," Callie said, hoping he would believe her.

"That took some nerve." Theo sounded overly impressed, Luke thought, especially since Theo never got in trouble or broke any rules.

Callie took off her jacket and Luke saw the camera around her neck.

"You're not supposed to bring a camera in here either," Luke said.

Grant turned around to look at her, frowning.

"It doesn't matter now," Callie said quickly. "We're leaving. And Agent Erickson was checking to see if it was okay anyway."

Luke watched out the window as they left the center of the camp and went down the road through the woods. Nothing moved as far as he could see. He supposed there weren't any Marines still patrolling around the trees. When the SUVs were only a few hundred yards from the gate, a flash of white caught Luke's attention.

"There's Comet," he shouted. "Stop, Adam!" Adam jerked back, startled at Luke's voice, but he kept going. Comet was racing through the woods in their direction, his tongue hanging out one side of his mouth, flopping up and down as he ran.

"Adam, stop!" Luke shouted again.

"Grant, tell Sal we're stopping for a few seconds to pick up the dog," Adam said.

Grant spoke into his microphone as Adam stepped on the brake.

"Sal says make it fast," Grant told Luke. "Don't get out of the car; just open the door."

Luke opened the door and called, "Comet!"

As soon as he heard Luke's voice, Comet barked. When he was a few feet away, he took a huge leap and landed on Luke's lap. Luke slammed the door as Comet danced around, licking Luke's face as if he hadn't seen him for a year.

"We're ready, Adam," Luke said. He wanted to put his arms around Comet and hug him, but he didn't want anyone to think he was being sappy. He grabbed the terrier's head between his two hands and ruffled his fur. "You mutt. Don't ever do that again. It's not worth getting in trouble for a cat."

Callie made a funny sound beside him, like she was trying not to cry. Callie never cried.

Luke scanned the woods for the cat, but he didn't see Tocho.

"I'm sure your kitten will be okay," Theo said. "The fire probably won't even come this far. It is extremely difficult to predict the path of a fire. There are so many variables."

"I don't want to talk about it," Callie said.

They were almost at the gatehouse. Both the inner electric fence's gate and the outer wooden gate were open, and Luke could see the kitchen vans and one of the Marine trucks disappear out of sight as they went out the gate and down the hill. The camp commander, Colonel Donlin, was inside the gatehouse, speaking into a phone.

Sal's car was already through the gate when Luke heard a rumble of engines. A big group of motorcyclists came up the hill too fast, speeding toward the gates. Some veered off into the grass, and some came to a screeching halt, nearly hitting Sal's SUV.

Adam acted quickly, swinging the car around in a sharp turn. Everyone was thrown to the side. Comet's toenails dug into Luke's legs and Callie fell against him. When the car was a couple of hundred feet from the gate, Adam maneuvered so they came to a stop, putting the Marines' vehicle in front of them. Luke turned around and saw that Isabelle had mirrored Adam's moves so that the trail car was still behind them.

Colonel Donlin came out of the gatehouse, motioning the Marines to go out the gate. Adam and Grant were talking to each other and into their microphones, their words so staccato Luke couldn't even tell what they were saying. The Marines went through the gate, stopped right behind Sal's vehicle, and poured out of the truck, lining up in front of the motorcyclists. The colonel went back into the gatehouse and the electric fence's gate shut, leaving the two SUVs inside.

"What's going on?" Callie asked. "Who are those people on motorcycles?"

"Probably just a group who didn't realize they were on the wrong road," Adam said. "Don't worry. We'll wait a few minutes until they move off."

"Are you sure they didn't come here on purpose?" Luke asked Adam. "When you swung the car around like that, I thought you were worried." He shifted in his seat, tapping on his leg, trying to see out the front window. It was hot in the car. Strapped in by the seat belt, he felt trapped.

"Just a precaution." Adam turned around and grinned. "Besides, I don't get to try that maneuver much."

"Luke, sit back," Callie said. "You're squishing me."

Luke moved away from Callie but couldn't stay still. He tried to see around the outside edge of Grant's seat, but only Sal's back was visible from that angle. If he could open the window, he would be able to get a better view, but he knew from experience the agents never allowed him to put his head out the window.

"Luke, I don't think anybody evil would wait outside the fence of Camp David to grab you just on the off chance a forest fire would make us leave," Theo said. "That's what you're worried about, right? That's what they told us at school before you started, about kidnappers and terrorists and stuff, to explain why the agents were there all the time."

"No, that's not it." Luke felt embarrassed that Theo knew what he was thinking. "Besides, nobody can break into an armored SUV," he added, trying to convince himself more than anyone else.

"One of them has a teddy bear strapped to his handlebars. See?" Theo said. "That's probably a good indication this isn't a terrorist group."

"Maybe they came this way because of the fire," Callie said.

No one had a reply. They all sat watching Sal wave his arms at the lead motorcyclist, a man with long gray hair and a leather vest. An armed Marine sergeant took up a position right behind Sal. Luke could tell it was Hector. Hector was taller and skinnier than most of the other soldiers.

Finally, the man held up his hands, as if giving

in. The motorcyclists revved up their engines and turned around, heading back down the road.

"We're clear to go," Adam said, putting the car into gear and moving forward. The electric fence's gate began to open again. When they were within fifteen feet of the guardhouse, a herd of deer ran out of the woods, leaping crazily as they headed right for the vehicles. One tried to leap over Sal's SUV but couldn't clear it. The deer's hooves pawed desperately at the slick surface until it fell back onto the pavement.

Comet went crazy. He leaped into the front seat and up toward the windshield, and then ran back and forth across the dashboard. In one motion Luke unbuckled his seat belt and started climbing into the front seat to get Comet, but he lost his balance and fell against Adam, just as the dog tumbled off the dash onto Adam's left arm, pulling Adam's arm and the steering wheel to the left. The whole car swung left and off the road as Adam tried to throw Comet off him, but Comet slipped down on Adam's feet.

The SUV sped up and hit the gatehouse wall, the heavily armored vehicle plowing through it easily. Pieces of stone and glass from the shattering gatehouse windows exploded up on either side. Luke heard a screeching sound as his side of the car scraped against the wall and he felt his body moving sideways through the air. His head smashed against Adam's headrest, his legs flying up, and his foot hit Callie or Theo; he couldn't tell which.

Theo yelled, "Callie!" but Luke didn't look back, because he saw an arm come up over the front of the car and he knew Colonel Donlin was falling beneath it. The air bags in the front seat burst open. Comet shot up and catapulted over him as the car jerked to a stop. Luke closed his eyes, trying to shut out the pain in his head. He heard sirens in the distance.

"You okay, Luke?" Grant asked. Adam was talking into his microphone to Sal.

"Yes," Luke said, pushing himself back. "The colonel . . . he . . ."

"I know," Adam said. "Stay put."

Luke looked at Callie. Blood was pouring out of her nose as she lay against Theo, who was staring straight ahead, his head tipped to the side, a puzzled look on his face.

"My door is blocked," Grant said. "I'll have to come out your side, Adam." He slid over and out the door.

Adam was already out, opening Theo's door. Luke heard a creaking sound above them, then a much louder grinding noise.

"Watch—" Adam's voice was cut off as part of the gatehouse roof came crashing down.

19

The Gatehouse

Horrified, Luke saw a beam hit Grant's shoulder. The agent collapsed under the weight, falling down out of Luke's view. Adam had disappeared too.

"Luke, are you okay? Can you climb out?" Somehow Isabelle was already partway in the car next to Theo. "Who is bleeding? There's a lot of blood. Luke, are you okay?"

"Let's get out," Luke said to Callie. "Isabelle, Adam and Grant need help."

"Luke, listen to me. *Are you hurt?*"

Isabelle's voice reminded him of something Sal had drilled into him: "In an emergency, listen to the agents."

"I'm fine," he said, trying to keep his voice

calm. "Callie's nose is bleeding because I think my foot hit her. We're all fine. Now help Adam and Grant . . . and the colonel. I saw him go down in front of the car."

"I will, but I'm going to help you first." Isabelle took hold of Theo's arm. "Come on out, Theo. Watch where you're stepping. Callie, tip your head back and pinch your nose," Isabelle ordered. "It will stop the bleeding."

"I lost my glasses," Theo said. "I think I hit my head. I lost my glasses."

"I didn't see what happened to Adam!" Luke said. "Where is he?"

"Luke, listen to me. The faster you all get out of here, the faster I can help Adam."

"I lost my glasses," Theo repeated.

"Can you unbuckle your seat belt, Callie?" Isabelle asked. Callie didn't move.

Luke took a deep breath. He knew Isabelle would insist on getting them out first. "I'll do it," he said. Callie's face was a mix of tears and blood. She kept wiping the tears from one eye, smearing more blood each time. He reached over her to undo the clasp.

The electricity was out and the fallen beams were obscuring most of the remaining windows of the three sides of the gatehouse still standing. He couldn't see anything but flashes of green trees and hazy sky though them.

"We need to leave the building before anything else falls." Isabelle took Callie's arm and guided her away from the car, and then reached in for Luke.

"I don't need help," Luke said. He climbed out, balancing on a pile of rubble, and saw Adam crumpled on the ground a few feet from the car.

"No!" Luke yelled, pushing his way around Isabelle and kneeling beside Adam.

Isabelle knelt down beside him. "He's breathing, Luke. I can see his chest moving. I think he got hit in the head when the beam fell and is just unconscious. Now you have to get out of the building. Someone will be here soon to help him and the others."

Luke bent toward Grant. The agent lay facedown, pinned by the beam resting on his back.

"Get up, Luke, and get out of here." Isabelle pulled on his shirt, nearly tipping him backward, and then when he didn't stand, she grabbed him under his arms and hauled him up. Theo was already scrambling over piles of stone toward the gaping hole made by the SUV. He tripped and fell to his knees, then picked himself up, shaking his head but not saying anything. Callie stood close by, staring at the debris, not moving. A beam resting on top of the rubble shifted, creaking, and then she rushed after Theo, little squeaks coming from her throat.

"If you don't go, I'll have to carry you," Isabelle said.

Luke felt his feet moving forward, picking his way carefully until he stumbled outside. The sunlight blinded him for a moment, and then he saw Sal on the outside of the electric fence. The gate was closed between them. The Marines stood in a group by their truck. Hector gave a thumbs-up to Luke, and even from where Luke stood he could see Hector's smile.

"Don't touch the gate!" Sal said in a loud voice that verged on a yell.

"Don't worry, Sal; we know it's electrified. Right?" Luke said, turning to Theo and Callie. He was alarmed by the blank expressions on their faces. "Are you guys okay?" Luke watched them closely.

"I think I bumped my head," Theo said.

Luke pointed at a nearby tree. "Maybe you should sit down until you feel better."

"Why is the gate closed?" Callie asked. "It was opening right before the crash."

"I'm not sure," Luke said, and then the image of the colonel came into his head. "The colonel had his hand on the gate lever when the car hit him. I think either he pushed it when he fell or something fell on it."

"I think I bumped my head," Theo said again.

"I think you did too. Callie, here." Luke pulled off his T-shirt. "Can you wipe your face?"

Luke didn't know whether Callie's head cleared at that moment, or the sight of his scrawny, pale chest shocked her back to life, but she straightened up and grabbed the T-shirt. At least she didn't laugh. When she was finished, she handed it back to him. Luke didn't want to put it back on. It was all smeared with blood, but he felt funny standing around without a shirt on. He pulled it over his head, trying to ignore the damp spots.

"Please, Callie, can you make Theo sit down?" Luke said. "He's acting so strange. I'm going back in to help Isabelle."

"Okay, Theo, come on." She took his hand and led him away. He went without a word.

"Don't go in there, Luke!" Sal shouted, reaching his hands up as if he wanted to grab the gate.

"I'm just going to go see what's happening. I'll stay outside." Luke turned around even as Sal continued to tell him not to move.

At the edge of the building Luke stopped, waiting for his eyes to adjust to the gloom inside. He saw Isabelle balancing on a chunk of stone by Grant's motionless body. She had her finger to the side of his neck.

"Is he . . . is he dead?" Luke called.

"No, he still has a pulse." Isabelle spoke into her microphone. "Sal, Colonel Donlin is alive, but he's trapped under the car. Grant is breathing but his pulse is very weak. It looks like at least an arm is broken. Adam is unconscious; I don't see any obvious injuries. I'm going to climb over and get the rubble off the gate control and try to reopen it. It looks twisted, from what I can see." Isabelle listened for a moment.

"Luke, you are making Sal a crazy man," Isabelle said. "Get back where he can see you."

"I should be helping." Luke fought the urge to go inside. "It was my fault." If he'd held on to Comet, none of this would have happened.

"I know you want to help, but right now the best thing for you to do is to go back to your friends."

112

"I think Comet is still in the car."

"Leave him for now. Please go outside."

Luke knew from the tone of her voice not to argue. "I'm just going to call for him while I walk out, okay? Comet! Comet!" When the dog climbed out the car and padded slowly toward him, he felt relieved. Adam moaned then, and anger surged in Luke. If only Comet had stayed still!

Outside, he didn't know what to do. He wanted to help, but he didn't know how. Callie ran over to him, motioning toward Theo, who was leaning against a tree trunk, his eyes closed.

"I think he's really hurt," she whispered. "He has a big bump on his head and he keeps repeating himself. We've got to get out him of here!"

"Don't worry," Luke said. "Isabelle is going to get the gate open."

"I really smell the smoke now. Don't you?"

Luke hadn't noticed before, but now he could smell it big-time, like it was a monster bonfire. "Yes," he said, fighting to stay calm. "But we'll get out of here soon. They won't leave us in here."

"It's a good thing you're important," Callie said.

"It's not just me," Luke protested.

"Sure," Callie said, turning away from him.

A park ranger drove up in a Jeep, his tires squealing as he came to a halt next to Sal's SUV. The ranger hopped out almost before the vehicle had come to a complete stop, and rushed toward Sal. Hector moved to intercept him.

"You've got to get out of here right now." The ranger's voice was loud. "Park Road is already cut off to the east, and the fire is getting out of control. It's moving fast because of the high winds."

"How many firefighters are on-site?" Sal asked.

"Not enough. Some of the crews were already on their way to help in Missouri." The ranger wiped his face. It was bright red, as if he had been running, and Luke could see the sweat stains on his uniform. "Why isn't that gate open? How are the firefighters supposed to get inside if they need to?"

Sal still had the same calm expression he always had, but Luke could see a trickle of sweat running down his face. Sal spoke into his phone. "We need the remote-access control to open the gate. We need at least two helicopters, one for Speeder and one for the wounded. Now."

"*You* are going to be cut off if you don't leave now," the park ranger told Sal. "You're out of time. The rest of the park is evacuated, and the way the fire is spreading, the whole place will be on fire in a couple of hours."

Suddenly a loud popping noise and a flash of light came from the remains of the gatehouse.

20

The Outer Zone

"Isabelle! Isabelle, do you copy?" Sal cried into his microphone. "Isabelle, come in." The expression on Sal's face changed, and Luke knew he didn't hear anything.

Luke didn't dare turn his head to the gatehouse. He didn't even want to breathe.

Finally, Sal spoke. "Luke, here's what I need you to do. Walk around to where you can see into the gatehouse. Do not go inside or touch anything. See what happened to Isabelle."

Luke went toward the gatehouse, feeling like he was walking in slow motion, not wanting to see inside. If Isabelle wasn't answering, he knew it would be bad. He came around the back of the car and peered through the gloom. It was very still. No Isabelle. Sal had said not to go inside, but he couldn't see unless he did. If she was hurt, he had to find her.

He climbed in over the pile of debris. Once inside, he still couldn't see Isabelle. A beam above him shifted, sending a shower of small particles down and dust up. He hesitated, unsure what to do next. A moan came from the front of the car. Luke crept forward, feeling sick to his stomach. He didn't know if he could make himself look in front of the car. He knew Colonel Donlin was trapped there, but he didn't know what to expect.

Bracing himself, he kept moving forward. Colonel Donlin lay propped up against the front wall of the guardhouse, inches from the front bumper. Luke couldn't see his legs. Isabelle lay in a crumpled heap, her body partly on the front bumper and partly against the wall. The moaning came from the colonel.

"Colonel Donlin, it's me, Luke."

The colonel opened his eyes. "I tried to tell her not to touch the lever, but she didn't hear me."

"What happened to Isabelle?"

The colonel coughed weakly. "The lever's

damaged. She touched it and got an electric shock. I was watching her; she lost her footing and her arm grazed it. The shock threw her back here."

"Is she . . . is she alive?"

"Yes, I can just touch her with my fingers and I think she's still breathing."

"I can reach her." Luke climbed over the hood of the SUV and reached down to touch Isabelle's arm. As soon as he did, he felt his fright drain away. He thought he could see her breathing.

"I can get her out," Luke said, excited.

"Luke, no," the colonel said. "I saw her head hit the wall when she fell. If she hurt her neck and you try to move her, you might make it much worse. Leave her until help arrives."

Luke climbed back over the car. "I'm going to tell Sal what happened."

Callie was at the gate talking to Sal. "What happened, Luke?" She sounded frightened.

"Isabelle got a bad shock when she touched the lever," Luke said. "She's unconscious, and the colonel doesn't think I should move her. The lever is damaged. We can't open the gate from here."

"We're working on that," Sal said. "There's some glitch in the software controlling the remote access, but we also have helicopters coming, Luke. They should be here soon."

Luke saw Hector come forward. "Sir," Hector said to Sal, "why can't we try to send a rope line across the fence? We could attach it to a tree on this side, and try to get it to catch on a tree on the other side. I know Luke can climb up those trees. Everybody knows he climbs like a monkey. He could tie it on the other side. I'll go across and help them back over."

"Sergeant, it's a good idea, but it won't work," Sal said. "We thought of climbers as a potential threat when the fence went up. The trees large enough to support a rope line were either cut down or pruned to prevent just that sort of attempt. If you try to use a tree that is too far back, the rope will sag right into the fence. If we had a launcher and a metal cable it might work, but we don't have either."

"Callie, how's Theo?" Luke tried not to flinch when he looked at her. With all the dried blood on her face, she looked awful.

"I can't tell," Callie said. "He's being quiet now. I don't know if that's good or bad."

Luke didn't know either, but he couldn't stand to just wait around for something to happen.

"I'm going in the gatehouse."

"Luke!" Sal sounded furious. "Wait." Most of the Marines were climbing back into the truck, and Luke saw Hector looking at him.

"Luke, the fire is getting very close. You'll have to move up the road just a short distance, away from the fence," Sal said. "Don't go too far. Stay on the road and the helicopter can land there to get you."

Luke thought he could hear a crackling sound. The air was getting hotter and thicker.

"What about you, Sal? You need to get out of here. The park ranger said you would be cut off." Luke didn't see the ranger anymore. He must have decided not to wait around.

"I'll go as soon as the helicopters get here," Sal said, taking out a handkerchief and wiping his forehead, now covered with sweat.

Theo came up to the fence, his watch in hand. He had tears running down his face but he didn't seem to notice. "It's bad. It's really bad."

"What do you mean, Theo?" Luke asked.

"We don't have much time. I've been thinking about it. We don't know how fast that fire is going to move, but it's not very far away because we can feel the heat and see the smoke. The woods aren't as thick inside the fence as the forest is outside, so it won't spread quite as fast here, but it won't slow down that much if the wind keeps up. We have to get out. Look!" Theo's last words ended in a choked sob as he pointed to the road behind Sal.

There was fire there, glowing red in the underbrush. The grass next to the road was sparkling with little bits of cinders and some of the trees were aflame. Luke knew Sal wouldn't leave the entrance as long as Luke was trapped inside, even if the fire came right up to the agent and consumed him. Luke was determined not to let that happen. He knew what he had to do.

21

The Quagmire

"Sal, we're going to the back gate," Luke said. "We're taking one of the cars. Send the helicopters there, because we're taking Isabelle and Adam and the colonel too."

"No! Just move up the road a little ways," Sal commanded. "You are not leaving here. You are not driving a car. It's too dangerous. That's an order. The helicopters will be here any minute."

"Sal, we're going," Luke said. "The fire is getting too close to you." He held up the chain around his neck, the disk on it shining in the sunlight. "If the helicopter gets here before we get there, they can find us by my locator disk. We'll see you soon. Come on, Callie!"

Sal's strangled "no" was the only sound Luke heard as he and Callie ran back to the gatehouse.

Callie knelt by the colonel and he opened his eyes.

"Colonel," Luke said, "the fire is getting closer, so we're going to the back gate. We'll move the car enough to free you, and we'll get Adam and Isabelle in the car Isabelle was driving. I . . . I don't think we can take Grant." Luke knew just by looking at the size of the beam that lay across Grant's back that it couldn't be budged. "Someone will come back for him as soon as we get the gate open."

"No, son." The colonel struggled to get upright. "You're never going to be able to move this vehicle, not with all the rubble in here. Don't worry about us. You need to get out of here, but you have to listen to me first."

"We're not leaving you, Colonel," Luke said.

"Please listen. It's hard for me to talk and you need to listen. The camp is in automatic lockdown. Do you hear the sirens?"

In all that had happened Luke had forgotten the sirens still wailing near the main buildings, their sound muffled by the trees between the gatehouse and the center of the camp.

"What does automatic lockdown mean?"

"Luke, Sal is calling you," Callie said.

"Will you go see what he wants?" Luke asked. "The colonel's trying to tell me something important." He didn't want to see Sal. Sal would just keep telling him what not to do. He heard Callie move away and turned his attention back to Colonel Donlin.

"The system thinks there's an attack on the compound and the fence has been breached. It has gone into emergency mode." The colonel stopped talking and drew a few breaths. "You can't follow the road back through the center of the camp and then out to the back gate. The inner perimeter defense ring is on and it cuts right through the road in two places."

"We're on the outside of the defense perimeter, aren't we? We're trapped between it and the electric fence." Luke sank back on his heels. There was nowhere to go and no one to help them.

No wonder Sal was so frantic.

Colonel Donlin roused himself.

"No, Luke, you're not trapped. Think. You know the woods are like a big band around the central zone with all the main buildings. Inside the woods, the defense perimeter beams are located so that they form a continuous circle. It's like an invisible fence. Do you understand?"

Luke tried to comprehend what the colonel was saying. Colonel Donlin knew Camp David better than anyone. He had been there for years. If anyone could get them out, it would be him. Luke thought about the colonel's words. Trying to focus, he put his finger down on a dusty part of the floor and traced the image forming in his head.

"I think I understand. Camp David is like a doughnut. In the center where the hole would be are most of the buildings, that's B, the woods are the doughnut itself, and the electric fence is the outside edge of the doughnut. The defense perimeter ring is like a thin ring of frosting. The main road cuts the whole thing in half, top to bottom. We're here." He wrote *FG* at the bottom of the circle, to stand for the front gate. "And we need to get here without going through the perimeter ring, the frosting." He wrote *BG* at the top of the circle, to stand for the back gate.

The colonel gave a gasp that might have been a laugh. "That's right. I never thought of it that way, but you're right. You won't get through the defense ring in the woods, and because the

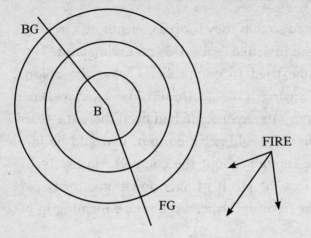

road goes through the ring in two places, you can't take the road. You wouldn't be able to tell which part of the road is protected anyway. The devices generating the perimeter are too well concealed."

"You said the defense system was a ring. Can't we just crawl under it? Is it aimed so it would hit someone who was trying to run through? Like a tape across a finish line at a race?"

The colonel coughed, his face gray. When he spoke again, Luke had to lean in to hear him. "Think of an invisible fence about ten feet tall and about a foot thick. There are hundreds of millimeter-wave-generating units positioned on the trees to create the wall. Every tree in that ring has two units, one on each side of the tree, and they're aimed at the trees next to them in the ring. A person can't crawl under it. It goes all the way to the ground. But there's another way."

"I get it." Luke understood exactly what the colonel was trying to tell him. "We go through the woods, around the outside of the ring to the back gate. We won't cross the defense perimeter that way."

"Right. The defense perimeter system is about a hundred feet outside the circular nature trail. I know you know where the trail is, but keep close to the fence, just to be safe."

"Can we get an SUV through the woods? We can't get Adam and Isabelle there any other way."

"I don't know. Maybe, but it would take some time to find places the car would fit between the trees. Luke, you need to get out. Don't worry about the agents. They wouldn't want that."

"I'm not leaving them. Besides, my friend Theo really hurt his head. I'm not sure how well he can walk."

The colonel was quiet for a few seconds. "Take my jeep. It's parked behind the gatehouse and the keys are in it. If any vehicle can get through the woods, it can. Don't go too fast, though. The

President will be pretty mad at me if you get hurt." He gave raspy sound like a chuckle.

"I'll be careful," Luke said. "But we can't just leave you here."

"I'll take my chances. Besides, it's my job to be the last one out." The colonel smiled a little. "Help will be here soon. The fire may slow down or go around us. They don't always do what you expect them to. And, Luke, I expect that jeep back in pristine condition. Not a scratch on it."

Luke felt like crying now. He knew the commander was making a joke so Luke would stay calm, just like his mom and dad did when things went bad. The colonel's jeep was almost a legend at Camp David. It was ancient, a huge old jeep with extra seats in the back, and so beat up, it looked like it had survived many wars, but the colonel always refused to give it up.

"Son, listen." The colonel beckoned to Luke to get closer. "There's a pass code to open the back gate if they can't get it open remotely. The whole system is in lockdown, because this gatehouse was compromised by the accident. You have to type in the override code; do you understand? The code today is four-nine-eight-three-two-eight. Can you remember? Four-nine-eight-three-two-eight. Say it back to me."

Luke tried to calm down enough to get it in his head.

"I can remember," Theo said, coming up behind Luke. "Four-nine-eight-three-two-eight."

"Are you sure? Is your head okay?" Luke asked.

"It feels like it might explode at any second, but I can still remember a six-digit number." Theo sounded angry, but Luke didn't want to take the time to find out why. "I want to find my glasses," Theo said.

"Go ahead. Can't we do anything for you, Colonel Donlin?" Luke asked.

"No, you need to hurry."

Callie brought over what looked like part of a chair cushion. "If we put this behind your back, you can sit up better, and you'll be able to breathe better." Luke pulled the colonel up slightly and slipped the cushion behind him.

"Now go," the colonel said. "That's an order." He tried to smile again.

"We'll hurry," Luke said. "As soon as we let them in the back gate, someone will come get you. Colonel, I think we should try to take Isabelle."

"No, son, she's . . . she's . . . Just go. . . ." The

colonel's voice trailed off.

Luke felt everything go fuzzy and dim, as if he were looking down a long tunnel at the colonel far in the distance. He reached out and grabbed the car door to steady himself, putting his head down on the window. It was cooler than the air around him, and it felt so good he didn't want to move.

"It's not fair," Callie said. "I didn't even want to come here in the first place. I want to go home." A tear ran down her face, making a stream through the dirt. She kicked at a piece of stone on the floor. "Ow!"

It was Callie's "ow" that steadied Luke. He straightened up. "We're taking Adam, at least. Theo, we need your help. Did you find your glasses?"

"Yes, but they're a little twisted, and one lens popped out. I can't find it. I have a monster headache."

"I'm sorry," Luke said. "Let's just get out of here so somebody can give you medicine for your headache."

"We're never going to be able to move Adam," Callie argued. "He weighs a lot. Luke, when I was outside I could tell the smoke is getting thicker.

The fire is moving farther up the road."

While Luke had been concentrating on Colonel Donlin's words, he hadn't even thought about the fire. Now he felt how hot the air was, and he could taste the smoke.

"We aren't leaving him, and I can't do it without you. Callie, you take his legs, and Theo and I will each grab under an arm." Theo mumbled something too softly for Luke to hear, but he did shift around to Adam's right side. Callie gave in and took her place at Adam's feet. When everyone was in place Luke said, "I'll count to three and we'll lift him. One, two, three. Now!"

They heaved Adam up. Theo was able to lift him clear of the ground, but Luke struggled to get him high enough not to scrape his body on the pieces of stone on the floor. Each step took too much time, as they tried to find level places to put their feet.

Adam's vest caught on a jagged piece of a beam and ripped.

"Set him down," Luke said. "Callie, can you pull it free?" Luke wished Adam would show some sign of life; even another moan would be encouraging.

Callie pulled on the vest and more of it ripped.

The roof creaked.

"I don't like the sound of that," Theo said.

"One big effort." Luke tried to sound unworried, but he took a quick glance up. "Colonel, we're leaving. Someone will be here soon." The colonel didn't answer, or at least Luke didn't hear him.

They struggled over the stones, and Luke knew Adam's back was scraping on some of them, but it couldn't be helped. It was like moving a giant, heavy rag doll, and none of them were strong enough to do the job easily. By the time they had him out of the building, they were all panting, trying to catch their breath. Sal still stood by the gate, watching them, yelling into his phone.

They hauled Adam into the back of the jeep. "Okay, we're ready to go," Luke said, trying not to panic at the crackling sounds from the road behind Sal. The smoke was getting thicker.

"Luke," Sal yelled, "get Adam's earpiece and microphone off him and use them so I can talk to you. I need to tell you how to avoid the defense system."

"The colonel already explained," Luke yelled back. "I've got it. Sal, get out of here. Theo, unclip the microphone from Adam's cuff; then if you take out his earpiece, you can pull out the wire that runs up his sleeve."

Theo was looking at his watch again. "I think the helicopter will be here in about ten minutes. We should wait."

"Sal will be dead in a few minutes if he doesn't move!" Luke screamed. He sucked in a breath of air to yell again, but the hot taste of the smoke made him cough instead. "I'll do it myself. I'm going, and Callie's going too, right?" He didn't want to look at Callie in case she agreed with Theo. "You do what you want." Luke got the microphone and earpiece without having to shift Adam around too much. He hoped all the moving they were doing wasn't going to make Adam worse.

"I don't want to just stand around," Callie said. "The helicopter will find us wherever we go, and I want to get farther away from the fire."

"Okay, I'll go." Theo climbed in the passenger side and buckled his seat belt. "I'm already having trouble breathing."

"What about Comet?" Callie asked. She was still standing by the jeep.

Luke hadn't even been thinking about Comet; he had been too worried about everyone else.

"He followed me out of the building. I don't know where he went. Comet! Comet!" When the dog didn't appear, Luke said, "He'll probably run after us once we start going. We have to leave so Sal will go too." Sal was the one in the most danger.

"You're so determined not to leave Adam behind," Callie said. "I'm not leaving Comet." She ran back to the gatehouse.

"Callie!" Luke pounded his fists on the steering wheel in frustration. "She hated Comet a half hour ago. I don't understand."

"Me neither." Theo took off his glasses and tried to straighten them. "But then, I don't understand any girls."

Callie came back carrying Comet. "He was lying by Isabelle's SUV. I don't know why he didn't come when you called him. I hope he's not hurt."

"We can't worry about that now. He has to sit in the back with you," Luke warned. "He's caused enough trouble today."

"Okay, okay, he's being very quiet anyway." Callie climbed in the back.

Once everyone was in, Luke glanced back at Sal and gave a strangled cry. Tendrils of fire were only feet away from the agent, advancing on him fast. Sal was still talking into his phone, staring at the fire as if he couldn't believe it would come any closer. Flaming leaves fell from the trees, the wind catching them and blowing them in crazy patterns. One hit Sal's shirt and he jumped back, trying to brush it away, but it disintegrated into tiny embers, speckling his hand. He jerked it back and turned to Luke, his face an unreadable mask.

"We're going *now*!" Luke yelled. "Run, Sal!"

22

The Back Gate

"Stay close to the fence!" Sal shouted as he plunged into the forest. Luke started the jeep and pushed on the gas pedal. The engine roared.

"Wait!" Theo said.

"What?"

"Buckle your seat belt."

In any other situation Luke would have laughed. Leave it to Theo to remember seat belts.

"Don't gun it," Callie said. "Just push on the gas a bit."

"I know, I know," Luke said. He handed Theo the microphone and the earpiece. "See if you can talk to Sal."

Luke knew how cars operated; he had just never

driven one. Taking a deep breath, he put the jeep in gear and gave it some gas. The jeep jolted forward and he pushed hard on the brakes.

"Let me drive, Luke," Callie said. "*I* can drive."

"No, I've got it. I was just getting used to it." He pushed on the gas pedal again, more gently this time, and the jeep moved forward. "Hold on," Luke said. "Since we can't drive on the road, it will be rough."

It was rough. Luke hadn't expected it to be so tricky to hold the steering wheel when the jeep bounced over a rock or an exposed root. It was hard to figure out how much to turn the steering wheel without going too far, and he threw himself and everyone else from side to side until he got the hang of it. He could still hear the sirens in the distance, but the sound was so constant, it was easy to ignore now.

"Why can't we go on the road? How is the helicopter going to land in the woods? I don't want to get lost in there," Callie said.

"We won't get lost. Camp David is like a big doughnut, with the road cutting it almost in half."

"What? A doughnut? What are you talking about?" Callie said.

Luke could picture the layout of the camp in his head, but he realized it would be hard to explain to Callie. She hadn't been here long enough to understand it easily. "We don't have time now. I'll tell you later. Just trust me," he said.

"Let me drive," Callie said. "I drive the pickup at the ranch. You sit in the back."

"No, I'm driving."

"Who made you the boss?" Callie said. "I'm sure I can drive better than you."

"Look, Callie, I know how to get to the back gate. You don't. And I drive the golf carts all the time." A golf cart couldn't be too different from a jeep, Luke thought. He wanted to add that he had no intention of moving out of the driver's seat, but he knew that would make Callie mad.

"Theo, what about Sal?" Luke asked, hoping Callie would stop arguing.

Theo put the earpiece in his ear. "Sal! Sal! Can you hear me?" he yelled. He listened for a moment. "Sal can hear me. He says I don't need to yell. He's following the fence around the outside to the back gate. He said we would get there before he does, so we're supposed to wait for him before we open the gate." Theo turned the microphone over in his hand. "One of the wires connected to the microphone is almost broken. I hope it holds together long enough."

Luke felt better knowing Sal was going along with the plan. As far as he could figure, it shouldn't take Sal more than twenty minutes to get to the other gate. It couldn't be more than a mile or two.

"I heard you," Theo said into the microphone. "Sal says we'll have to get out in an open area once the helicopter gets here."

"They'd better hurry," Luke said. "I've been in enough of them to know they don't do so great in fog, and the smoke is getting worse fast."

Theo wasn't listening. "Sal says they're going to put your dad through in a minute. He's on Air Force One. Stop so I can give you the earpiece."

"No, just hold it up to my ear." Luke felt as if the fire were really chasing them now. If he stopped, he was afraid something terrible would happen.

Theo shook the earpiece. "Something went wrong," he said. "Sal, I can't hear you anymore. Are you there?"

"Did you lose the connection?" Luke slowed the jeep.

"Sal, are you there? I guess we did lose it," Theo said. "Sal just said to hold on for a minute; then there was a noise, then nothing."

"Maybe when they tried to patch my dad through to Sal's frequency, something went wrong. Just keep listening. With all the equipment they have on Air Force One, they can let my dad talk to anyone anywhere."

Adam gave a loud moan from the back. Luke looked back to see Comet, sitting in the backseat, licking Adam's face.

"Adam, can you hear me?" Callie asked.

Luke didn't hear a response. "Is he waking up, Callie?"

"No, his eyelids moved but they didn't open. Does anybody else notice it's getting darker? I didn't know it would get darker." Her voice was small again.

"I think we should keep moving," Luke said. He didn't like the darkening sky either. "The helicopter is on its way and I have my locator disk. We'll see Sal in a few minutes anyway."

"What about just using a cell phone to talk to Sal?" Callie asked. "Or is that too normal and not high-tech enough? Who has a cell phone?"

"I do," Theo said, "but not here. They wouldn't let me bring it. You have to have security clearance to have cell phones here."

"Wait, we should get Adam's phone," Luke said. "All the agents have satellite phones, so his should work no matter what. Callie, it's in his vest. We can call Sal, except I don't know what his number is." Luke had never had a reason to call Sal.

"We can just dial nine-one-one," Callie said. "That's what regular people do in an emergency."

"Okay," Luke said. "Where's Adam's phone?"

"I can't find it," Callie said. "Part of a pocket is ripped. I think it fell out when we were moving him."

Luke stopped the jeep, all of a sudden uneasy that they couldn't talk to Sal.

"It's at the gatehouse. We should go back," Theo said.

Behind them Luke could see the smoke thickening.

"No, we don't need it. We have the code. You remember it. Right, Theo?"

"Of course I remember it. It's four-nine-eight-three-two-eight. How open is the ground around the back gate? Can the helicopter land there?"

"They can land on the road either right inside or right outside the gate. They've cleared the trees just like at the front gate, and those pilots can land in really small areas."

Luke put the jeep back in gear. This time, he did a better job of steering, even though he still had to fight to keep the vehicle from swerving too much or hitting anything too big.

"Luke, why is there more smoke in front of us? I thought the fire was coming from the other way." Callie's voice trailed off. She was right. The sky in front of them was starting to get as dark as the sky behind them.

"I don't know. The back gatehouse is right up ahead." They came over a small rise and Luke pushed on the brake so quickly he felt like he was going to fly over the windshield. Outside the back gates they could see fire in the distance, treetops blazing, sparks jumping and dancing in the air. A pine tree caught fire with a loud popping sound, exploding like a huge firecracker.

"What's the fire doing here?" Callie screamed. "It's not supposed to be here. What are we going to do? We can't use the road!" She climbed out of the jeep and ran a few feet toward the gate and then stopped. "Luke!"

Luke didn't understand how the fire had gotten here. The back road ran out of the park to the northwest. If the fire started in the east, it shouldn't be on this side of Camp David.

"It's weird the fire is here too," Luke said. "It shouldn't be."

"Well, it is," Callie snapped. "I hate this place." Luke knew Callie was really frightened now, because those were the times she tried to cover her fear with anger.

"I think fires started in more than one spot because of the earthquake. Fires are the most common danger from earthquakes after the initial damage." Theo looked around as if he had lost something. "I wish I had my notebook. I could draw a map."

"What good would a map do us?" Callie pounded on the hood of the jeep. "What's wrong with you two? You act like you're not even scared."

Luke realized he hadn't thought that much about being scared. He had been so busy concentrating on his plan, he guessed he hadn't had time. Besides, he knew his dad and Sal would figure out what to do.

"This is really not good," Theo said. "I don't know if anyone can get through the fire to us."

"Don't just sit there. I don't think the fire is all the way to the gates yet. The wooden fence

143

isn't on fire. We can open the gates and get out ourselves." Callie pointed back behind them, the way they had come. "We know there's fire that way." She pointed in front of them. "And we know there's fire that way, so we go this way." She pointed out to the left. "What way is that?"

"It's sort of southwest," Luke said.

"Well, there isn't any fire there yet that we know about. Once we get through the gates that way should still be clear, and we can go through the forest until we find somebody. Let's go."

"Callie, it would be really hard to get the jeep through the forest. They don't clear out all the underbrush like they do inside the fence, and Adam can't walk," Luke said.

"We'll leave him here and go find someone to help him. Come on, Theo. Let's open the gate."

"I'm not leaving Adam."

"Theo, go on," Callie said. "You're the one with the code." Theo was out of the car and inside the gatehouse before Luke could stop him.

"Wait," Luke yelled. Now that they were here, he didn't feel as sure of himself.

Theo stuck his head out the gatehouse door. "What?"

"Sal told you to wait until he got here." It was

strange for Luke to move around without any agents nearby. They had been with him so long, like some sort of human armor all around him, he hadn't ever thought about how it would feel without them. He tapped his fingers on his legs, uneasy.

"Sal!" Luke yelled. "Sal!"

"What are you doing, Luke?" Callie said.

"Sal should be here by now. Sal!"

"Come on, Luke." Callie bounced up and down. "Let Theo open the gate. We don't need Sal here for that."

Maybe he should let Theo open the gate, Luke thought. It was just a gate, and the forest on the outside was almost like the woods on the inside. He could stay inside with Adam until Sal and the helicopter arrived, and Callie and Theo could go through the woods in case the fire spread too fast. He shouldn't keep them trapped here. They didn't even know Adam, and the fire was getting closer.

The fire was now about two hundred feet down the road, a wall of swirling colors and smoke. If he hadn't been able to feel the heat, Luke thought it wouldn't even seem real. For a moment he envisioned the fire stopping as it reached the fences, sputtering out against the force field of safety they formed. But he knew the fences couldn't really stop the fire; the wooden one would catch quickly, and the fire would go right through the chain link.

"Okay," Luke said. "Do it, Theo!"

23

The Woods

A thumping sound worked its way into Luke's head like a headache without any pain. He rubbed his forehead, trying to make the sound go away, and then he realized it was coming from the sky.

"I hear something." Luke climbed up on the hood of the jeep. "Can you see anything?" He pointed to the north.

Callie climbed up beside him. "It's the helicopter," she said excitedly. "Theo! I can see it . . . them. There are two of them. Here we are!" She waved, and Luke could just make out an outline in the smoke. Theo came out of the gatehouse.

Luke felt like a weight had dropped off him. "They can land on the road," he said as he jumped off the jeep. "I'm going to unbuckle Adam."

As the helicopters drew closer, Callie kept waving as if they needed to see her to find them.

"Those are Chinooks," Luke said. "The army uses them for rescue missions."

"That would be what we need," Theo said.

The helicopters drew closer, and they all waved, needing to do something. Comet put his paws up on the backseat and barked. The lead helicopter adjusted its path, turning in their direction.

"They know we're here!" Callie jumped off the jeep and ran down the road. Luke couldn't believe the sense of relief he felt, almost like sinking into a soft bed when he was really tired. In less than an hour they would be back in Washington, D.C., away from all this, and everything would be back to normal.

The wind from the helicopter's rotors created a funnel of smoke and leaves beneath it as the helicopter started to descend. Another pine tree outside the fence exploded, sending out a cloud of flames. The flames rolled up and up, engulfing the helicopter as if the fire were trying to swallow it. The helicopter disappeared from view, emerging a second later, twisting to the right. The other helicopter swung to the side and it looked like it was going to get clear, but then the rotor of the first hit a wheel on the other.

"Get out of the way!" Luke screamed. He flung himself at Callie and Theo, both standing transfixed at the sight of the helicopters tangled together. "Run! Run! They're going to crash." He grabbed Callie's arm and dragged her with him away from the helicopters, not wanting to look back.

The boom sounded and he felt a surge of heat washing over him. Callie pulled him to a stop. Both helicopters were down. An enormous fireball rose over the trees as the fire spewed out in all directions, fed by the fuel in the helicopters. Luke couldn't even see if there was anything left of them. The fire was too intense.

"We have to help the people in the helicopters!" Callie shouted. "Come on, Luke!"

"No, Callie." Luke felt his whole body clench. "Nobody could survive that kind of explosion." He fought back the tears, looking around for Theo, and spotted him on his knees holding his head. Luke started toward him and then saw the grass light on fire feet away from the jeep. Luke ran forward and tried to stomp it out, but the grass was too dry and there were too many little sparks coming from the bigger blaze, landing all around him.

"Callie, help Theo. Keep moving away," Luke yelled. "I have to go back and get the jeep."

"Open the gate before the fire gets to it!" Callie shouted.

"I have to move Adam away from the fire first. It's too close. You and Theo open the gate."

Luke jumped into the jeep and started the engine, trying to put it in gear at the same time. The engine made a grinding sound, but then slipped into gear. He turned the jeep and drove it back into the woods, away from the fire, and then stopped, trying not to think about the people in the helicopters. He climbed out and jogged over to Theo, who was still on the ground. Callie came running back from the gatehouse.

"That's not the right code, Theo. Try to remember." She called to Luke, "He fell down and threw up, and now he says he's not sure what the code is. Do you remember?"

The numbers wouldn't come into Luke's head. He tried to picture Colonel Donlin telling him the code. "It started with a four," he said, "and it had some nines and eights in it. What did Theo say it was?"

"Four-nine-eight-nine-two-eight."

"That sounds right," Luke said. "Are you sure you punched the numbers in the right way?"

"I tried three different times," Callie said. "Why didn't you let Theo open the gate when we could? This is all your fault!"

"Theo, think. Are you sure that's the code?"

Theo took off his glasses and cleaned the one lens on his filthy shirt. "I think so. I wish I could talk to my mom. My head really hurts. You know, when I'm sick my mom lets me watch as much television as I want."

Why was Theo thinking about television now? Luke rubbed his eyes. They were watering and itching from too much smoke, but the rubbing only made it worse.

"I wish I could talk to my mom," Theo said. "I wish I had my cell phone."

"Let's try a different code," Callie said. "Maybe it's just a little off. You said it started with a four."

"Okay. Theo, keep trying to remember if that's the right code." Luke went into the gatehouse. The back gatehouse was much smaller than the front gatehouse, but it had the same gate lever and a keypad next to it.

"What should I try?" Luke asked, glancing out the window. The fire was close, already in the nearest trees on the other side of the road. If they didn't get the gate open soon, the whole area would be covered in flames.

"Try four-nine-eight-two-nine-eight," Callie said.

It didn't work. Luke punched in as many variations as he could think of using those numbers but nothing worked. Why hadn't he tried to remember the number? He shouldn't have expected Theo to be the only one who could remember a number!

"Luke, the fire is getting too close. Don't you feel it?" Callie said.

The front edge of the fire was just feet from the door, and the metal keypad was getting hotter and hotter. He tried another number. Nothing. Another.

Callie took the hand he wasn't using. "Come on, Luke. I'm sorry I said that about Theo and the gate. You can't just keep pushing numbers while the gatehouse catches on fire."

"It is my fault!" He pulled his hand away. "You're right. We would be out of here by now." The keypad was so hot, he felt like his fingers were blistering every time he punched a number.

"Go ask Theo if he remembers something else."

"No, Luke, we have to get out of here." Callie took his hand again and pulled. "Let's go call for Sal."

Luke let her lead him outside. Callie called a few times for Sal, but he didn't answer. Luke knew he wouldn't. Something had happened, something bad. Sal would never leave him alone this long. What were they supposed to do now? Luke looked over at Adam, but Adam wasn't moving. Luke closed his eyes, but he could still see the fireball. This wasn't supposed to happen to him.

The fire came right up to the door of the gatehouse. He knew the stone walls wouldn't burn, but he didn't know how long the wooden beams in the roof would last, and with everything burning around him, Luke didn't even really care. He was too tired to care.

"Why isn't the electric fence off already?" Callie asked. "I thought Sal said they were going to try to turn it off remotely somehow. What if it's already off?" Callie and Theo both looked at Luke.

"It hums when the power is on," Luke said. "It's hard to hear, though. I can't hear anything with all the crackling of the fire."

"I'm going to find out." Callie ran down the fence line away from the fire. She stopped and then moved farther down the fence. When she came back, he could tell from her face the fence was still live.

"Why don't they turn it off?" She turned on Luke as if he should know, but he didn't know. It should be off by now.

"They would have to send a signal from Washington," Theo said, "either via satellite or underground cable or wireless, to the command center at Camp David to tell a computer there what to do. Something must be wrong with whatever system they're trying to use."

"That's a big help!"

"You asked," Theo said, shrugging his shoulders. "Luke probably knows more about it than I do."

Both Theo and Callie looked at him then like he was supposed to do something. No one had ever expected him to decide things. He was used to everyone else making his decisions for him, twenty-four/seven. Except that wasn't quite right. He had decided they should go to the back gate. Even though it hadn't worked out, Colonel Donlin had acted as if it was a good idea.

Luke tried to think. What was his dad doing right now? Did his mom even know what was happening? *Yield not to misfortunes, but rather go more boldly to meet them.* He could almost hear his father's voice.

He said it aloud. "'Yield not to misfortunes, but rather go more boldly to meet them.' Theo, what ancient guy said that?"

"Said what?"

"'Yield not to misfortunes, but rather go more boldly to meet them.'"

"Uh, that ancient guy would be Virgil."

"Right," Luke said. "Virgil. We aren't giving up. That's our motto. I don't want to just sit here anymore. Let's get back in the jeep, go to the command center, and shut off the electricity to the fence." He felt a surge of energy at the idea of something to do.

"Are you crazy? How are we going to do that?" Callie said. "I heard the colonel. He said that the defense system was activated and we shouldn't go back through the woods to the buildings. Those are the boxes on the trees you were so hysterical about, aren't they? The ones that zap you dead."

"They don't zap you dead. They just make you

feel like you're on fire," Theo said, putting his glasses back on.

"Wonderful. That makes all the difference." Callie glared at both of them and kicked the jeep tire. She looked like she wanted to kick Luke and Theo.

"I've been thinking about that. I think I have an idea. The colonel told me about where the defense perimeter is. It's supposed to keep out people on foot who are trying to sneak in, not armored vehicles or anything."

"So what good does that do us?" Callie said.

"You know, if they really are like lasers or microwaves, you should be able to block the beam," Theo said. He made a scribbling motion with his hand like he was drawing a diagram.

"What blocks a beam like that?" Callie asked.

"It depends on how strong it is. Something solid, like a piece of metal, if it's not too powerful," Theo said. "If it's really strong, it's hard to stop."

"They call it a millimeter-wave system, so it has to be more like microwaves," Luke said. "Those are blocked by metal, just like a microwave oven." Luke eyed the jeep.

"Then why can't we just drive the jeep through,

and duck down behind the doors?" Callie asked.

"The beams come from overhead," Luke said. "They would still get us."

"Even if we had one of the SUVs, we don't know if the waves will go through glass."

Luke took hold of one of the jeep doors. "But we've got metal right here. We can take off the doors and use them to block the beams, like armor, while we crawl through underneath them."

"That might work," Theo said, "except we can't be sure the doors will cover us completely. I'm a lot bigger than you two." Theo made more drawing motions with his hands. "This might be a terrible idea."

"We can't see the beams, right?" Callie said. "I'm not using some sort of crazy jeep armor and just crawling through hoping we won't get zapped. Maybe we should move back from the fire when it gets closer, and someone else will get here soon to help us."

"No," Luke said. "We don't know how long it will take for another helicopter to get here, and this other fire is spreading fast now. At least back toward the buildings in the center of the camp there shouldn't be any fire yet. It *will* work." He almost added, *I think*, to the end of that sentence, but he didn't want them to doubt him.

"Luke's right. I don't want to stay here." Theo climbed back in the jeep. "Try not to bump around too much, okay? I feel like I might throw up again."

"Okay," Luke said.

"I'm guess I'm in too," Callie said reluctantly, climbing in the back with Adam and Comet. "Just remember, if we get fried, this wasn't *my* idea."

24

Passage

Luke drove slowly, trying to get his bearings. It was harder than he thought to estimate where the nature trail would be, and to stop the right distance away from it. Usually, when he and Adam went running, they picked up the trail right outside Laurel Lodge, but now he was coming at it from the opposite direction. Finally he hit the brake, not daring to go farther. "We should be close. Can you hear the sirens are louder now? That means we aren't too far away from the center of the compound. I know where they've been pruning lots of the trees too. I bet that's where they put the boxes."

The three of them got out, Comet jumping

down too. Luke was glad they had moved far enough away from the fire so they couldn't hear it anymore. It made him able to concentrate better.

"Now what?" Callie asked. "How are we getting the doors off anyway? That can't be easy."

"First we get Adam out, because it's going to be rough." Adam mumbled a little when Theo started to pull him out, but even though he didn't open his eyes, he wasn't a total deadweight. He shuffled forward, leaning on Theo, while Luke tried to take some of his weight from his other side. When they lowered him to the ground, propping him against a tree, Luke knelt down in front of him.

"Adam, Adam, we need you to wake up. Adam, please." Once the words were out of his mouth, he couldn't stop the tears. He choked and crouched down on the ground, covering his face, knowing he was shaking, but trying hard not to make a sound. Without Adam and Sal, he was nobody, just a kid who didn't know how to do anything. How was he supposed to know what to do? Maybe they should just stay in one spot, hoping someone would come get them. He could hear his dad's voice: *Make haste slowly*. But that advice couldn't help now. What was he supposed to do? The whole thing was his dad's fault. They would never be here if his dad hadn't wanted to be President.

"Luke, come on, let's try your idea," Theo said. "The sooner we do this, the sooner we can get help for Adam."

"Go away," Luke said.

"I'm with Theo," he heard Callie say. "Come on, Luke. Get up."

Luke wished he could shut out the sound of their voices. He waited, his hands still over his face, expecting Callie to call him a baby, but she didn't. They didn't say anything else. Luke didn't know how long he crouched there all scrunched up, but then he felt Comet licking his ear. Luke reached his hand out and ran it along Comet's back. At Luke's touch, Comet barked and jumped around him, trying to lick his face.

"Luke, we don't have much more time," Theo said. "Look at the air."

There were bits of ash swirling about them now, like gray snowflakes in a winter storm.

"A helicopter won't be able to get through this, will it?" Callie said, moving over to Theo. He put his arm around her.

"We don't need a helicopter." Luke got up, not looking at either one of them, focusing on the jeep as a way to stop thinking about everything else. "I'm not going to just sit here. I don't care what my dad says."

"What do you mean?" Callie asked. "Why are you talking about your dad?"

"Never mind. It's just something he says that I don't think is always a good thing. You guys stay back. We don't have any tools to get the doors off, so I'm going to back the door into a tree and see if that works. Keep Comet clear too."

"You can't drive fast enough to break the door off. You'll be hurt when the tree hits the door," Callie said.

"He doesn't have to drive fast." Theo let go of Callie and picked up a rock about the size of a plate. "If we wedge the rock in the space between the open door and the car, the bolts may break more easily even with just slow pressure. Just make sure you put on your seat belt."

Luke felt terrible knowing he was going to do a bit more than putting a scratch on the colonel's jeep, but he didn't see any other way. Once Theo had the rock in place, Luke positioned the jeep about five feet in front of the tree, put the car in reverse, and stomped on the gas. The door hit the tree and the jeep jerked forward. Without thinking, Luke put on the brake. When the car stopped he could see the door was still attached, even though it was sagging from the frame because one of the bolts had snapped.

"The rock won't go back in," Theo said, examining the door. "There's no place left to wedge it."

"I'm going to have to run it into the tree again, faster and from farther away," Luke said. Callie opened her mouth, but then closed it again. Luke was glad; he didn't think he could stand too much more.

"Move back." He positioned the jeep about ten feet in front of the tree, put the car in reverse, and stepped on the gas, all as fast as he could so he wouldn't have time to think. The door hit the tree, the jeep jerked forward, and Luke's seat belt dug across his neck, gagging him.

"It's off," Callie yelled. "It worked."

Luke almost wished it hadn't. Now it meant he had to do it again for the other door. The skin on his neck was burning from the seat belt. How come people on TV never acted like it hurt when they fell or ran into things?

The second time he had to hit the tree twice

as well, and the muscles in the back of his neck screamed when he hit the tree extra fast to make sure the door would come off. He sat back and closed his eyes for a moment, wishing that had been the last thing he had to do, instead of just one of the first things. He wished he could erase the past few hours and go back to the morning, to being excited to show Theo the garage, and to joking around with Adam. After today, he didn't know if he could go back to that Luke.

"Now what?" Callie asked. "These doors aren't big enough to be like a knight's armor that covers you all up."

"I know," Luke said. "We're not making that kind of armor. We're going to hook them together, and prop them against each other to make sort of a tunnel we can crawl into. The beams are only about a foot wide, so we will be safe going in and out."

"I don't know." Callie knelt down and examined the doors. "They're awfully small. Are you sure we are going to fit?"

"I think I'm too big." Theo picked up one of the doors and held it to his chest. It looked small against him.

"We have to try," Luke said. "Now I need

something to hook the two together."

Theo set down the door and poked around in the back of the jeep. "We don't have any rope. There's nothing in here at all."

"Yes, there is, but the colonel isn't going to like it." Luke took out his pocketknife. "We'll use a seat belt and thread it through the door handles."

"You can't cut off a seat belt!" Theo objected.

"We don't have another choice." It wasn't as easy as Luke thought. His pocketknife wasn't very sharp, but by a combination of sawing and pulling, the seat belt came free. Luke picked up one of the doors. "Grab the other one, Callie, and then let's move forward. We'll wait till we get close to put the doors together. It won't be so heavy that way."

Callie picked up the other door. "How do we find the boxes?"

"We walk forward really slowly, until we spot one of the boxes. Theo, you should follow behind us. Without both your lenses, how well can you see?"

"Not very well. I'll stay back. Watch out for the jagged edges on the doors where they broke off."

"Then can you carry Comet? I know he won't

165

stay if I tell him to, and I don't want him to run ahead of us."

"Sure." Theo scooped up the dog and fell in behind Luke and Callie.

They edged forward, holding the doors in front of them like shields. The doors were heavier than they looked and Luke had to keep adjusting his hold.

"This isn't my idea of fun," Callie said.

"Well, it's not mine either." Luke couldn't see anything up in the trees. Each time he took a step, he stopped, waiting for something to happen to him, feeling his skin prickling.

"If it gets us, how long will we feel like we're on fire?" Callie asked.

"I don't know. I think the pain is supposed to be so great people pass out from it. That way they just can't run through it, feel terrible for a few seconds, and then get over it so they can keep on going."

"Great. Whoever thought this defense system up is one strange, sick person. How big do you think the boxes are?" Callie whispered.

"I don't know," Luke whispered back. "Why are we whispering?"

"It just feels like we should."

They continued to move forward, straining to see something, anything that might look out of place.

After a few minutes, Luke said, "I don't see anything. Maybe they aren't on after all, and we've just walked through the area."

"Wait! We can use my camera like a telescope. It has a twelve-x optical zoom. Here, Theo, take the door." Theo shifted Comet under one arm and grasped the door with his other hand while Callie pulled the camera off her neck and opened the lens. She looked through the viewfinder, scanning several trees.

"Nothing, no . . . that's just bark . . . no . . . wait." She moved the camera back to one of the larger trees and held it there. "It works. I see one!" She pointed ahead.

"I can't see it," Luke said. All he could see were the leaves fluttering on the trees from the hot wind.

"Right there where the branch forks. It's on the forked part going up. It's painted to look like the branch, but it doesn't match exactly. Just like when you look for lizards in the desert—you have to look for the pattern that's a little bit off."

"I still don't see it."

Callie went around behind Luke and put her arm up over his shoulder. "Follow my finger. Do you see it?"

"Yes, I see it!" The box was about the size of a DVD case, but thicker, painted a mottled brown. Callie was right; it didn't match exactly. The easiest part of it to see was the glint of the lens.

Theo caught up and Luke pointed to the box. "I don't see it," Theo said.

Luke moved as close as he dared to the tree, pointing upward.

"I guess I see it," Theo said. "I wish I had my other lens."

"I found the other box," Callie said. "I even see the little opening where the beam comes out."

"Okay, good." Luke tried to sound happy, but he almost wished Callie hadn't found the boxes. Maybe his idea was too crazy after all. He sighed, setting down his door. He took the other one from Theo and positioned them on the ground so he could strap the two together. "Callie, will you help me hold them so I can get them fastened?"

Callie grabbed one. "How are they going to stay propped up?"

Luke wound the seat belt through both door handles and pulled them together as tightly as possible, jamming the cut end back through the buckle. "They will hold each other up, kind of like when you make a card house out of two cards, the upside-down 'V' kind, except we'll have to balance them just right so there isn't a gap at the top where the rays could go through. The seat belt will help keep them together."

He took the doors and tried to flip them over to demonstrate, but they were too heavy. "Here, Callie, take one side and help me turn them the right way. We'll try it away from the rays to see if it works."

It took a couple of tries to get the doors over and positioned so they would stand alone. Callie knelt down and peered in. "That's a very small tunnel."

"It's all we've got," Luke said.

"Are you sure it won't fall down?"

Luke reached out and gave one door a slight shake. It wobbled but didn't knock the other over. "Looks good. Try it," he said.

Callie lay down on her stomach in front of the opening. "I think I can pull myself through using my arms and my feet." She slid forward using an inchworm motion. "This really hurts my arms, and my feet aren't doing much good," she called, her voice muffled.

"Keep trying," Luke said. "It's not very far."

Luke saw her legs move and then heard an "Ow!" Callie's body jerked up. The tunnel tipped to the side, bringing one door down on her back.

"That didn't feel so good. So much for that idea," she said, scrambling free.

"Sorry." Luke pulled the doors back up. "I should have stabilized them. If we hold them, it should work. Why did you yell?"

Callie held up her arm and pointed to a cut. "I dragged my arm across a rock. This isn't going to work."

"Yes, it will," Luke said.

"Luke!" Theo held out his watch. "I'm having trouble doing the math about the speed of the fire, but we'd better do something soon. Fires don't stand still."

Luke took a deep breath. "I'm going first."

25

The Barrier

"I should probably try first," Theo said, "you being the President's son and all. You shouldn't do it."

Luke was surprised to hear Theo volunteer. "Don't get all noble or anything," he said. "I'm a lot smaller than you, and this is one time when that's a good thing. I'll take up less room, and if anyone can get through it will be me." Neither one argued with him. They all stood there until Luke said, "Well, no sense waiting around."

He dragged the doors over as close to the trees as he dared, propping them back up. "I hope this beam really is only a foot wide. Callie, help me shove these into place."

Callie reached her hand out and then drew it

back. "What happens if we push it too far and the beams hit our hands?"

"That isn't going to happen," Luke said, trying not to imagine the feeling of his hand burning up. "Brace them for me, okay? Theo, you'll have to help too. Callie can hold one side and you can hold the other."

Once the doors and Luke were in place he had to will himself to inch forward, trying to ignore the rough ground scraping on his knees and his arms. It was the hardest thing Luke had ever done, waiting for the pain that might hit him. He hadn't ever thought about pain before. It was just something that happened, usually when he did something stupid, and he knew it would go away. This was different, knowing he could be jolted by something so intense, he wouldn't be able to stand it. The crawling seemed to take forever. Finally, he heard Callie's voice.

"Your feet are clear, Luke. I think it's safe to stop."

Luke realized he had been holding his breath. "No problem." He tried to keep his voice steady as he got up.

"Callie, why don't you go next?" He was impatient to get moving now. They were so close.

Callie took a few tiny steps forward and Comet started to follow.

"No, stop, Comet, sit," Luke said in his sternest voice. For once, Comet decided to obey, but Luke didn't know how long he would stay in one spot. "We'd better get Comet through before you. He's more likely to stay still if he's closer to me. Theo, put him down right in front of the doors." Luke lay down on the other side, peering through. He hoped when Comet saw his face, he would crawl through toward him. At first, Comet just sat there, his head tilted to one side, eyeing Luke.

"Here, boy!" Comet looked puzzled, sniffing at the doors. "Here, boy." Luke tapped the ground in front of him with his hand, and Comet came in far enough for Luke to reach in and pull him the rest of the way out. He set the dog down and picked up a stick, tossing it a few feet away. "Good dog! Go play with the stick."

When Luke turned back he noticed Theo's face was a funny color, really pale and greenish. "Callie, I think Theo should come next so you can hold the door on that side. Theo, are you ready?"

"I guess," Theo said.

"Maybe Theo should just stay here," Callie suggested. "I'm not sure the tunnel is big enough for him. We can come back and get him when we get Adam, right?"

"No!" Theo's shout startled everyone. "I don't want to stay here by myself. I think we should all stick together." He got down on the ground.

"Theo, wait, you might get stuck halfway through," Callie said, as Theo put his head into the tunnel. "Are you sure you want to try this?"

"Just hold the doors," Theo said. Luke's grip was so tight his fingers hurt as Theo edged through so slowly, Luke thought he would never be clear.

"You're doing great," Luke said. Theo's head was out of the tunnel when his glasses fell off. As he reached for them, his shoulder bumped the door Callie held and the whole tunnel shifted.

"I don't think I can hold it!" Callie yelled.

Theo stopped dead, his face flat against the ground.

"Try!" Luke ordered, putting his shoulder against the door he was holding. He reached his hand over Theo's head to grab the other door. "I got it! Go, Theo!"

Gasping noises came from Theo, and Luke was afraid he wouldn't move. "Just a little farther," he said, and Theo began to ease forward.

Just when Theo had made it through, loud

174

popping noises came from the east, and a faint roaring sound. A hot, steady wind and the smoke had caught up to them.

"Callie . . . ," Luke said.

"I know. You don't have to tell me to hurry."

Callie wriggled through so fast Luke didn't even have time to tell her to be careful.

"So much for the high-tech defense system," she said, standing up and brushing off her shorts.

Luke released his hold on the doors and got up. Comet, the stick in his mouth, nudged against his leg, like he wanted to play a game. The dog danced to the side. Luke bent down to grab him, but Comet dashed back toward the trees, right at the beams. Callie screamed and Luke lunged for the dog, grabbing hold and then throwing himself to the side. Luke collided with the ground, but the impact made him lose his grip on Comet. The dog went up in the air, and then came down, striking the edge of one of the doors. His body fell to the earth, hitting hard. He lay motionless.

26

Out of Place

"Comet," Luke yelled, moving over to pick him up.

"Is he okay?" Callie asked.

"I don't know." Comet opened his eyes halfway. "I think he got the wind knocked out of him." Luke set him back down, but he didn't move.

"We need to go, Luke," Callie said.

"I'll carry him." Luke got up and took the dog in his arms. Comet gave one tiny whimper and then fell silent. "Don't worry," he murmured. "We'll be out of this soon. Okay," he said more loudly. "We need to go this way, to get to the main road to the center of the camp."

Once they came out of the woods, they picked up speed, jogging down the road, past deserted buildings. Luke's shoulder hurt from taking the impact of the fall, and he felt pain in his knee every time he came down on it, but he didn't care anymore. The only noise was the sound of the sirens coming from various buildings, louder now that they were close. As he tried to get his breath in the hot, smoky air, Luke shifted Comet to a different position. The dog felt as heavy as a Saint Bernard instead of a twelve-pound terrier. He could tell Comet was breathing. When would he open his eyes again?

"I have to walk," Theo said, slowing down. "My head is really hurting now. I wish we could shut off the sirens."

"This is kind of like a horror movie." Callie shuddered. "Like when people come into a town and there's nobody outside, and they don't know what they will find behind any of the doors, and it turns out to be vampires or zombies. No, that's too creepy. Forget I said that."

A sudden scrabbling sound made them all jump.

"It's just some raccoons," Luke said. Five raccoons scuttled across the road, not more than a few feet away. A sixth animal climbed out of a tipped-over garbage can, following after the others. None of the raccoons paid any attention to them.

"They're trying to get away too, like all the other animals," Callie said. "They know the fire is coming. It's probably inside the fence now down by the gatehouse, isn't it? And it's inside the fence at the back gate. How are they going to get through the beams and outside the fence?"

"They aren't," Luke said. "The small animals live inside the fence all the time." *And they'll get burned up,* he thought, but he didn't say it out loud. "The big animals, the bears, were all moved out when the electric fence was put up. There was one that kept climbing up over the outer fence wanting to get back in. They had to keep tranquilizing it to move it out again."

"Maybe it was that bear I saw this morning," Callie said.

"You saw a bear?" Luke asked. "Inside the fence?" That would be all they needed, a bear as well as a fire to deal with.

"No, it was outside when we were driving up. I took a picture of it. I'll show you once we're out of here."

"I don't need to see it," Luke said. He was scared of bears, really scared of bears, ever since he had read a story where a bear attacked a camper in a sleeping bag.

"Why is the wind blowing all the time now?" Callie asked. "Maybe it's going to rain and put the fire out."

"No, the fire is creating its own windstorm," Theo said. "They do that when they get big enough."

Luke rubbed his face, feeling little bits of ash on it.

"So what's the plan?" Theo asked.

"We'll go through Aspen Lodge down into the basement to get into the command center," Luke said. "Come on, Aspen is right over there."

When Comet wiggled in his arms, Luke felt a surge of joy.

"Are you ready to walk, boy?" Luke asked, putting him down again. "You're pretty heavy for a worthless mutt." Comet took a few faltering steps, and then stopped, wagging his tail.

"Come on then," Luke said. Comet lay back down on the ground.

"Let's go." Luke took a few steps, thinking Comet would try to follow, but the dog made no attempt to move.

Worried, Luke said, "Okay, okay, I'll carry you

again." Luke held Comet close as he led the way. He hoped the air-conditioning was still on inside. It would be nice to get cool. Just as he was about to reach for the door handle, Comet raised his head and growled.

"He sees Tocho!" Callie exclaimed. She pushed past Luke. "Tocho!" She reached out for the kitten.

The entry area had a roof over it, shadowing the ground, but Luke saw a dark spot on one side of the door, and then he saw something move on the other side, a rope uncoiling.

"Wait!" Luke grabbed Callie to stop her. "Comet isn't growling at Tocho. Look on the other side of the entrance. There's a snake there, a copperhead, I think. It must be trying to get away from the fire too." Luke let go of Callie to get a better hold on Comet.

The snake was curled up in one shadowed corner, the narrow slit eyes focused on Tocho, its tongue flicking in and out as its head moved back and forth. The kitten stood in the other corner, his back arched, his fur so fluffed out he looked like a hissing, spitting ball of yarn.

"How dangerous is it? Is it like a rattlesnake?" Callie asked.

"Adam said a kid might die from a bite if he wasn't taken to the hospital, and even once at the hospital, the bite would be really, really painful. If one bites you on your hand, your whole arm swells up."

"That's dangerous enough for me," Theo said. "Is there another way in?"

"Yes, let's go around to the back door."

"Wait a minute!" Callie said. "We aren't just walking away to let Tocho be a snake snack."

"It's not safe to pick up the cat." Luke motioned at the snake and the snake's head turned toward him.

"We have to leave him," Theo said.

Callie ran down the steps, looking around at the grass and the flower beds. "At the ranch once, I saw one of the ranch hands move a rattlesnake out of a horse stall. He didn't want to scare the horse in the stall, so he took a long forked stick and picked the snake up with it. We need to find a forked stick. Don't they have any sticks here?"

"The gardeners pick up all the sticks," Luke said. "We'd have to go back into the woods."

"No, I have a better idea. Wait here." Theo disappeared around the side of the building in a lopsided jog.

Callie looked back at the cat. "It's okay, Tocho."

"He's pretty brave for being so little," Luke said.

Callie crooned soothing words to the kitten until Theo came back around the corner carrying the robot and Luke's laptop.

"Here's your snake catcher," he said, handing the robot to Luke.

"That toy is going to catch a copperhead?" Callie rolled her eyes. "It couldn't catch a ball sitting still on the ground a few hours ago."

"It's not a toy," Luke said. "But Callie's right. The grabber arms don't close far enough. The snake will slither right out."

"They might, if we change the program and download it." Theo sat down on the sidewalk and opened the laptop. He punched the on button once, and then when nothing happened, he punched it again.

"It's dead. I think I left it on," he said. "We have to charge the battery."

"We don't have time." Luke looked behind him again. "Callie, I'm sorry. We need to get moving. Maybe the snake will leave. It's probably too scared to be thinking about eating Tocho. We'll check on him once we get things working inside."

"Snakes don't just bite because they're hungry," Callie said. "I have an idea. The robot's batteries are still working, right? It's just the computer battery that's dead. Theo, I need your socks."

27

Beyond Reach

"What?" Theo asked. "My socks?" He sounded very confused.

"Yeah, those things between your feet and your shoes, which I'm sure are very smelly at this point. Take them off. I mean, just take off one. I only have one hair band." Callie pulled the hair band out of her braid.

"Why my socks? Why don't you take off your own?"

"Will you just do it? You have the biggest feet, so you have the biggest socks. I'm going to wrap your sock around the claw and fasten it with my hair band to make the opening smaller. Then the robot will be able to hold on to the snake."

"I guess that might work," Theo said doubtfully, sitting down on the ground and pulling off his shoe. He pulled off his sock and held it out. "It's wet. My feet have been sweating."

Callie took it between her thumb and her forefinger. "Yuck!" She handed it back to him. "I'll just tell you what to do with it. Wrap it around one of the claws like you are making a bandage. Okay?"

"Where's the whistle?" Luke asked. "We can't control the robot without the whistle."

Theo pulled it out of his pocket. "I stuck it in my pocket when Comet went after Tocho."

"That's good," Luke said, putting the robot down a few feet from the snake. "Everyone back up in case the snake gets mad."

"You can bet he's going to get mad. If you had a plastic pincher toy making beeping noises and coming at you, you'd be mad too," Calllie said.

"Wait, Luke." Theo backed away, handing Luke the whistle. "You should do the controlling. I can't see well enough to know when to signal the extensors."

"Callie, I need you to take Comet," Luke said.

"Okay," she said, coming back up the steps and taking the dog. "Please don't let that snake get Tocho."

"I think we should all be ready to run if the snake gets away." Theo wavered a little.

"Let's just do this." Luke blew the whistle and the robot lurched forward. The snake's head turned toward it. Now that his eyes were adjusted to the dim light, Luke could see the flat, triangular shape of the snake's copper-colored head as it extended slowly toward the robot.

It was going to be a lot harder to grab the copperhead than he thought. The snake's head and neck would move too fast. Luke decided it would be easier to grab the snake's curled-up section, so he blew the whistle to stop the robot until he could figure the best angle.

The snake's head went back toward Tocho.

"It's attracted to movement," Callie said. "Move the robot fast, so it will stop looking at Tocho."

"No, that's good," Luke said. "We don't want it to see how close we're getting."

Luke blew a short burst and the robot moved to within a few inches of the snake. Attracted by the motion, the snake flicked its tongue out steadily as its head moved back and forth between Tocho and the robot.

"I remember something I read," Callie said. "Snakes smell with their tongues. He's confused because the robot doesn't smell alive. Stop moving the robot until he forgets about it. Snakes can't have all that many brain cells, so it should only take a minute. Then just make the robot get him."

Callie was right. After only a few seconds the snake turned its head back to Tocho. Luke signaled the robot to move forward and then again to close the claws. The claws caught the snake on one of the coils and the snake struck at it over and over, struggling to get free.

"It's not going to hold!" Theo shouted. The snake tipped the robot back and forth as it whipped around, so that it looked like the robot was fighting too. "If the controller hits the concrete and breaks or one of the cables comes loose, the claw will release!"

"Callie!" Luke yelled, not daring to look away from the snake. He wished Callie had found a stick they could use as a weapon if the snake got away from the robot and came toward them. Throwing a whistle at it wouldn't do any good, and he doubted he could use his pocketknife against it. "Go get that garbage can. Dump out the garbage and bring it up here."

"Theo, take Comet." She plopped Comet down

on the ground, ran to the garbage can, and dragged it over to Luke.

Luke picked it up, trying to get a good grip. It was heavier than he thought, but his movements stopped the snake momentarily as the reptile's head swerved around to see the new threat. Luke heaved up the can and it was on top of the snake before any of them could blink.

"I promise," Callie said to the kitten as she scooped him up, "when we get out of here you're never going to have to go outside again, if you don't want to."

There was a sound like distant gunshots. Luke flinched, grabbing on to the stair rail.

"It's more trees exploding," Theo said.

"Let's get in the building," Luke said. He picked Comet back up and edged around the garbage can. "Will you bring my laptop, Theo? Maybe it will be safer inside."

Callie pulled on the door. "It's locked."

"I have a code," Luke said. He punched it in and they opened the door, feeling the air-conditioned air flowing out. Only the emergency lights were on, and with the darkness it felt like night inside. It was quiet too, the sound of the sirens muffled, and Luke suddenly realized he could breathe better in the smoke-free air.

"This way," Luke said. "With any luck, we'll get the fence off in just a few minutes."

They ran down the stairs until they came to the door at the bottom.

"There's the keypad," Theo said. "It's a lot higher up than the intercom. That's weird."

"I hope my code works for this one too. I've never tried it." Luke put Comet down.

The code didn't work. He tried again, pulling on the door. Nothing happened.

"Use the code Adam used this morning," Theo said.

"I don't remember the code," Luke said. "That was just a Secret Service access code they use to tell each other it's okay to open doors. It changes every day."

"Do you remember it, Theo? Try it anyway," Callie said.

"It was three-eight-one." Theo punched it in. Nothing happened. Theo examined the keypad again. "I know why it's so high. That's a retinal-scan-access reader," he said. "You have to both have a code and then be in the system so it can read your eye."

"What do you mean?" Callie asked.

"It scans a person's retina. A retina is as unique as a fingerprint. Since we aren't authorized, we aren't going to get in there."

"Scan your retina, Luke," Callie said. "Maybe you're in the system."

"No, I'd remember if anyone had ever said, 'Let's scan your retina, Luke, so you can get in restricted areas.'"

"Can't you at least try it? How do you know what kind of information they have about you, anyway?" Callie said.

"Okay, I'll try. Theo, you're going to have to boost me up so I can get my eye level with it. It's made for taller people than me." Luke put Comet on the floor.

Theo didn't argue either. He just knelt down and clasped his hands together for Luke to step on them. It didn't do any good. The scanner gave no sign it recognized Luke.

"Well, then Tocho and I are going back upstairs," Callie said. "It's creepy down here, and I'm getting claustrophobic."

"Me too," Theo said. "We aren't making any progress down here."

"Wait, maybe we shouldn't go." Callie had taken only a step forward when she stopped. "Can't we just stay here? Wouldn't we be safe down here if the fire came over us?"

"Who knows?" Theo said. "Fire consumes all the oxygen around it. It sucks it in from every direction. I don't know if this area would hold on to enough oxygen for us. Plus, it's likely to get so hot in here we wouldn't survive, but if there's no other choice, I guess we'll have to try."

"Not such a good idea then." Callie headed back up the stairs.

"Maybe we would be safe in the swimming pool," Luke said. He looked to Theo.

"Maybe, I don't know. The water is going to be very hot. I've read forest fires can make the water boil in streams."

Luke didn't want to imagine that. "The pool is a lot deeper than a stream," he argued. "Let's go look." He picked Comet up and they went back up the stairs, out the door, and around the building.

Callie had already found the pool. It was only half-full, bits of ash floating in it.

"This may be an obvious question," Callie said, "but where's the water?"

Luke knelt down on the edge. "I see a crack in the bottom. It's leaking out." He walked around to the steps, thinking hard. "I'm going to wash my face off, at least. Maybe Comet will feel better if he has a drink."

"Pool water isn't good for dogs," Theo said. "It has chemicals in it."

"Dying of thirst isn't good for dogs either," Luke said. "A little can't hurt him." He carried the dog down and placed him where he could lap at the water. At first Luke just splashed water on his face, and then decided it felt so good he dunked his whole head in.

"Move out of the way," Callie said. "I want to do that too." She plunged her head in the water and came up smiling. Some of the drips fell on Tocho, and he struggled to get out of her arms.

"Not again," Callie said. "I'm holding on to you too well now."

"How about you, Theo?" Luke asked. Theo was sitting on one of the lounge chairs.

"My head hurts so much I don't want to bend over."

"Are you okay?" Luke asked.

"I feel kind of sick. I think I might throw up again."

Luke cupped his hands and scooped up some water, trying to make it to Theo before it all spilled.

"Here, take this and rub it on your face."

"I'm thirsty," Callie said, "and I bet Theo is too. There has to be some water or something to drink around here."

"Water would help us all think better. Maybe it would help my headache too." Theo lay back in the chair like he was sunbathing.

Luke used the edge of his shirt to wipe his face. He thought Callie looked better with some of the blood off her face.

"The pool house." Luke waved to the small building on the other side of the pool. "There's a little refrigerator right inside there. It should be full of drinks." Now that Callie mentioned water, Luke realized his own throat was so dry, it felt painful to swallow.

Callie went in and came right back out, empty-handed. "The floor is collapsed and the refrigerator is down in some sort of pit."

"What? It must have happened during the earthquake. Can't you just reach down and open the door?" Now Luke couldn't wait for water.

"I said it's in a pit, way down. I can't reach it."

"Why would there be a pit under the pool house? Let me look."

28

Underground

Luke took a few steps and Comet tried to follow, wobbling with each step. "No, boy, you stay here," Luke said, worried the dog still couldn't walk right. Comet dropped to the ground, panting, and Luke hurried after Callie into the pool house.

"There." She pointed.

"It *is* a pit," Luke said.

"I said it was a pit."

"That's weird. It must have happened during the earthquake. Open those curtains so I can see better." Luke pulled at one of the broken floor pieces. "I see stairs." He pulled another board up. "Wait, I think I know what this is. These are old bomb shelter stairs! I bet that's how people were supposed to get into the shelter before the tunnels from the buildings were built. They must have covered the stairs when they built the pool. That's amazing. I never knew they were here. They have to lead to the command center. Theo!" He pulled away more flooring, the wood splintering in his hands.

"I'm right here," Theo said.

"I need your help with these boards."

Between the two of them they pulled up enough to make an opening.

"I'll go first," Luke said. He eased himself down, trying not to brush against the bits of broken wood. When he touched the concrete step, his foot slipped. "Be careful; the stairs are wet."

When they were all down, Theo said, "This must be some of the water from the pool. I can't see very well."

"Let me go before you," Callie said. "Take my hand." Tocho was clutched in the other, eyes closed, purring so loudly even Luke could hear.

At the bottom there was a short corridor that ended at a metal door.

"Is it locked?" Callie asked. "I don't see a keypad."

"I think this is too old. It was probably boarded

up before they had keypad-entry doors." Luke pulled on the handle. The door screeched and gave a little. "I don't think it's locked; it's just warped. Theo, can you pull too?"

The door came open with an earsplitting screech.

"What's behind it? It's really dark down here," Theo said. Luke was glad to hear that his voice sounded better.

"It's a wall," Luke said. "They walled up the other side of the door."

Theo put his hand on it. "It's just plasterboard, and it's wet at the bottom. I bet we can push through." Theo shoved, and the board shifted. "There's probably some kind of office furniture on the other side of the wall. Everybody push."

Something crashed on the other side as they pushed their way through, bits of plasterboard crumbling under their hands. Theo fell forward onto a shelving unit that now lay on the floor. There was water all over the floor. Luke climbed across the shelving.

"How about some lights?" Callie found a switch on the wall.

The room they found themselves in was a

storage room, full of metal shelves stuffed with blue plastic binders.

"This room isn't going to do us any good," Luke said. "Let's find the computers."

Callie opened another door. "There are computers in here," she said, "and there's another door."

Theo and Luke followed her. She had already opened the second door. "Look down those steps," she said. "That's where all the pool water is."

Luke could see into a small room, down a few steps off the main room, computers lining three walls. The water was up over the keyboards, as if people had been using their laptops in a Jacuzzi and forgotten them.

"Those computers are goners," Theo said. "When the water came in, they shorted out. That's probably why they can't turn off the fence remotely. Maybe one of those was supposed to receive the signal."

"Maybe," Luke said. "I don't know exactly what those computers did in that room. But this one is the main security ops room." It looked different without any people in it. Luke's attention was caught by the bank of screens on one wall, showing images of different places around the compound. He moved closer, trying to figure out what parts of the camp he was seeing. Most were of buildings and views of the woods, but some of the screens were just black. Luke had a sinking feeling about those. Some of the cameras must be burned up.

A screen at the bottom flickered and Luke leaned in closer. It was of some part of the woods and the back of a building. Luke couldn't tell which building. It wasn't one of the main lodges; at least, he didn't think it was. There were sector numbers scrolling across the bottom of the screen, but they didn't mean anything to him. To his horror, he watched as fire appeared in the woods, creeping toward the building.

"We need to hurry," he said, turning away. He didn't want Theo or Callie to see. If either one of them panicked now, they wouldn't have a chance.

"Okay, so is the switch in this room?" Callie swung around.

"What switch?" Luke asked.

"The one that turns off the electric fence. Isn't that why we came here?"

"There isn't going to be some big switch on the wall with a sign on it that says, 'Electric Fence.'"

"Now you tell me. What are we doing then?" Callie waved her arms around the room. "I thought we went through all that trouble to shut off the fence."

"There's some computer station here that controls the power to different parts of the facility," Luke said. "We just have to figure out which one."

Theo sat down at one and moved the mouse to bring the screen back. "Luke, we have a problem. I bet they're all going to want passwords to access them. Try them."

Luke and Callie tried one after another. Every single one said, ENTER PASSWORD.

Luke sat down in a chair, exhausted. This was one hurdle too many. He should have realized they would never get into a password-protected government computer. Hackers might be able to, but they didn't know enough to know where to start. He laid his head on the desk, wishing he could just close his eyes and go to sleep and wake up when it was all over.

"Does your dad have a password? Do you know it?" Callie asked. "I know my dad's password for his laptop, and I would think the President would be able to access everything."

"Dad wouldn't want access to the computers.

He barely knows how to use one."

"We have to try something," Callie said. "At least try. Try some word, like 'camp' or 'David' or something."

"Callie, nobody who's good with computers ever uses obvious passwords."

"I'm going to try anyway. You never know; maybe somebody got lazy. Here, hold Tocho." She plopped the cat down in Luke's lap and then sat down at the closest computer and typed something, then hit "enter." "I guess that isn't it. I'll try something else." She typed more words, hitting "enter" each time. "Uh-oh." Callie swung the chair around. "Now it's flashing, 'Access denied.'"

"If you enter the wrong password too many times, it locks you out," Luke said.

"Just because I couldn't get into this one doesn't mean I can't get into another." Callie tried them all, until every one flashed, ACCESS DENIED.

"Callie, Luke's right. We'll never get in," Theo said. "These computers are as secure as any in the world." Theo sat back, slumping in his chair, mirroring Luke's dejection.

"Are you both just going to sit there?" Callie's voice rose. "After all this! Are you going to let a bunch of machines beat you?" Callie hit her fist against a desk, shaking the computer on it. She let out a whoop. "Wait. Why can't we just try something simpler? They're all just machines. They all run on electricity. Why can't we just unplug them all, and then whichever one is sending a signal to the gate will be shut off?"

Theo frowned and then smiled. "That's a great idea. It might work. They're all plugged into docking stations, so just pull them off. That should disconnect them."

Callie removed one. The screen dimmed, but the computer stayed on. "I forgot about the batteries," she said. "We need to get all the batteries out." Theo already had one upside down. When he popped the battery out and turned the laptop back over, it was dead.

"It's working! Help, Luke," Callie said.

"There's another problem, Theo." Luke pointed to a large station. "This computer console is hardwired into the wall. We can't unplug it, and I bet it's the important one. They wouldn't use laptops as the main computers."

"Can't we just cut the cord?" Callie came over and examined it.

"How are we going to do that without electrocuting ourselves?" Luke asked.

"Wait," Theo said. "There has to be an emergency off switch to this console in case something shorts out and starts a fire. I read about how there used to be big red buttons on the front, but on newer mainframes they aren't in such obvious places, because people used to push the buttons accidentally. I bet this is it." Theo pointed to a small switch under a plastic cover.

"Turn it off," Callie said. Theo lifted the cover and hit the switch. The sirens went off, and then the lights went off. It was as dark as a cave, except for one emergency light by the door.

"I never want to hear another siren again," Callie said. "Do you still have Tocho?"

Luke reached out to hand the cat to her as the lights came back on.

29

The Front Line

"No!" Callie yelled.

Theo sighed, slumping down again. "There must be a backup power source in some room here. The cord for the console probably runs back into a server room, and I bet there's another room beyond that with the backup. I've seen something like that at my dad's office. Those rooms would all be locked. They really limit access to those rooms."

"We have to try to find them. There have to be off switches there." Callie was already moving around the room.

"It won't do any good," Luke said. "I forgot there's an emergency generator too, and there's no way we can get to it. Nobody can climb the fence around it without getting sliced to pieces. It's a special kind of reinforced barbed wire." He was angry now. It was almost like Camp David was some sort of devious enemy, thwarting them at every step. He had played computer games like that, feeling like he was never going to get to advance. He wasn't going to let that happen here.

"Don't say anything, Callie. Here, take Tocho back." He didn't want to hear her complain. "I'll say it for you. I know I have been really stupid, not thinking things through." She started to talk but Luke held up his hand. "Let me finish. I'm not going to be beaten. You keep coming up with ideas that are smart because they're so simple. Well, I've been thinking of an idea too. Some of it's simple; some of it is not. And I'm making up a saying of my own; it's not Latin, but it's going to be my new motto: 'Have lots of backup plans.'"

"What's the idea?" Theo asked, rummaging around on someone's desk until he found a piece of paper and a pen.

"I don't have time to explain it all. I think the inner perimeter defense system is off. The sirens are off, so that's a good sign. The system is new;

it takes a lot of power, and the generator is old. I think the generator is just controlling the emergency lights and the electric fence."

"Are we just supposed to take your word for that?" Callie said.

"You'll see. I'll prove it to you," Luke said. "But first we need some supplies. A lot of supplies. And a truck."

"Are you sure you're feeling okay?" Callie asked. "What good is a truck going to do us? We can't get through either gate."

"We don't need to," Luke said. "Come on, we need water too. Let's get that refrigerator open." This got them moving back into the storage room to crawl over the shelving to the old corridor.

Callie reached the refrigerator first. "This water had better be cold." She pulled open the door. The refrigerator was packed with soft drinks and bottled water.

"Let's take as many as we can carry," Luke said. "We don't know when we'll get any more." When they got back outside, Theo sat down on the ground.

"I need to rest for just a minute," he said. "I'm really sleepy."

"Here." Callie put Tocho down and opened

a bottle of water, then handed it to him. Luke opened his and poured the cool water into his mouth. Nothing had ever tasted so good. Tocho went over to the pool where Comet was still lying down. The kitten squeaked at him and Comet wagged his tail, being friendly.

"If you two had done this hours ago, you would have saved us a lot of trouble," Callie said, getting down near the kitten. She cupped her hand and poured some water in it, and Tocho lapped it up.

"I hope Adam is okay," Luke said. "We should get moving again."

"When can we have those ice-cream sundaes?" Theo asked. "That would taste really good right now." He had his watch out again. "My watch isn't working. I don't know what time it is."

"What?" Luke thought Theo's voice sounded kind of droopy.

"You said we were having ice-cream sundaes. I wondered what time we would have them. I was going to bring us the doughnuts we left in the tree house but there were ants on them. My watch isn't working."

Luke didn't know what to say. "We'll have ice cream tonight, Theo. Come on, I saw they forgot to put away one of the golf carts. We can take that."

"You go on. I'll just stay here and take a nap."

"No, you can't stay here." Theo was scaring Luke now. "You have to get up."

Callie touched Luke's arm, tipping her head as if motioning him away from Theo. He followed her a few feet away.

"I think he has a concussion," she said in a low voice. "The same thing happened when one of the ranch hands fell off the roof of the stable. Aunt Kate said people with concussions get sleepy and confused."

"What are we supposed to do?" Luke said.

"I don't know exactly. Aunt Kate was the one who took care of the ranch hand. I didn't do anything. We should get Theo out of here as fast as we can, though. Let me try something." She took a bottle of water over. "Theo, please drink some water. It will make you feel better." She put the bottle in his hand and Theo took a drink. "Come on, if you don't go with us, you won't be able to have a sundae." She took one of his arms. "Get up."

Theo did what she wanted. He heaved himself up and stood as if he were waiting for her to tell him what to do next.

"I'll help Theo to the golf cart, but you should get Comet," Callie said, picking Tocho back up.

Luke went back down the steps of the pool and got Comet. He scratched the dog's ear. "I hope you can walk soon, you mutt."

They went around to the front of Aspen Lodge. "The golf cart is parked in the big lot by Laurel Lodge," Luke said. "I saw it when we walked by."

"Where are we going?" Callie asked when they were settled in the golf cart.

"I need to get some stuff from the maintenance garage."

"Isn't that going to be locked too?"

"It isn't some sort of reinforced building. It's old, and besides, there aren't any weapons or anything important in there, so it's not going to have a complicated lock."

They were at the garage in only a minute or so. Luke pulled up in front of the big sliding double doors.

"Theo, you can stay here," Luke said, hoping Theo wouldn't fall asleep. "Callie and I will get the doors open."

"Theo, drink some more water." Callie set Tocho in the seat. "Watch Tocho for me, okay?"

Tocho curled up in a ball, yawning. Luke was amazed neither animal seemed aware the fire was coming.

"Okay," Theo said.

"Good." Luke saw that Comet had his head on Theo's knee. "Callie, you're going to need both hands to get all the stuff. Come on, we need to go around to the back."

The back corner of the garage was a small office with windows and doors to both the main part of the garage and to the outside. As Luke expected, the outside door was locked.

"Stand back," he said, picking up a rock. Giving Callie time to move away, he heaved it at one of the windows and the window broke with a satisfying crash.

"Score one for Luke," he said. "I'm going to win after all."

"Can I help?" Callie asked. "I've always wanted to smash a window on purpose."

"Go for it," Luke said. Callie picked up another rock and hit at the remaining panes of glass.

"I'll unlock the back door once I climb through," Luke said. The window wasn't as free of glass as Luke had thought, and one sliver cut into his palm. He didn't even care anymore. There wasn't time to think about little things like cuts.

Callie pounded on the door, and when Luke opened it, she rushed in. "Luke, there's fire behind the garage. We have to get out of here."

Luke looked out to the west and saw flames over the tops of the trees. "The fire is spreading faster over there because the helicopter was full of fuel, but we still have time, if we hurry." The keys to the landscape trucks hung on the wall right where they were supposed to be, and Luke grabbed a set.

"First thing we need to do is get the doors open. This way." They raced past the landscape trucks, the golf carts, and the lawn mowers lined up in neat rows. Luke unlocked the main doors as quickly as he could. He took hold of one, shoving hard, until it slid open.

"Theo, we need you!" Callie called. "We've got to hurry!"

Theo climbed out of the golf cart and walked to them, looking more awake now. Comet lifted his head, then laid it back down. Tocho didn't stir.

"How do you feel?" Luke asked.

"I feel better after the water. What are we doing?"

"We need to load up this truck." Luke motioned

to the one closest to the doors. "I'll lower the lift to make it easier." He climbed up into the cab, put the key in the ignition, and then hit a switch. The back lift came down.

"They use it to load up the lawn mowers," Luke said, climbing out of the truck. "We're going to use it to load all our stuff. Theo, you get a metal chain. There should be some big ones the landscape crew uses to pull shrubs out of the ground. Get the biggest one you can find and put it in the truck. Callie, go get that golf cart, the two-seater, and drive it over here. The one we've been using is too big."

"Oh, so now you trust me to drive?"

"Golf carts are easy," Luke said. When he saw her frown and clench her fist, he backed up. "Wait, I didn't say that the right way. I trust you to drive. I'm sorry, but we don't have time for you to be mad at me, okay?"

"Okay, I guess."

"When you're done, we need lots of rope, strong rope. It's all hanging on the wall behind the trucks. Bring all the thickest rope you can find. And then—"

"Wait, wait, let me get this stuff first," Callie said. "Breathe a few times."

Luke did. "I'm going to get some scrap two-by-fours and some sledgehammers."

Once everything was in the truck, Luke stopped to think. He snapped his fingers. "I forgot the most important thing. We need a big block and tackle, one with all the pulleys already put together on it, and they're really heavy. Callie, bring the golf cart to the back of the garage, where the tools are. We can load it in the golf cart instead of carrying it."

The block and tackle was so heavy, Luke wondered if his plan was going to work after all. The metal garage was hot on a normal day, but now it felt like they were inside an oven, baking, and he decided he didn't have any choice. The plan would have to work.

Once the block and tackle was on the lift, Luke snapped his fingers again.

"The only other thing I want is a creeper. Callie, can you get one back by the tools? Get a big one."

"What's a creeper?"

"Oh, it's one of those flat carts with wheels that mechanics use to wheel themselves under the car. Wait, I'll get it myself, because I know the one I want. Theo, you get in the truck. Callie, you're going to follow us in the golf cart back to the jeep."

"What about the boxes in the woods?" Callie said.

"They're turned off, I'm telling you. The emergency generator doesn't have enough power to run them. I'll prove it to you. Put Comet and Tocho in with Theo. They'll be safer. Now, I need to get the creeper."

He found it right where it was supposed to be, and rode it over to the truck like it was a skateboard, remembering how he used to drive Adam and Isabelle crazy doing that. He didn't want that thought, though, so he pushed it away. Once the creeper was in the truck, he raised the lift and climbed in the cab. Comet was sitting in the driver's seat.

"Move over, boy," he said. "We have work to do, and this time we are going to get it done."

30

Surrounded

"Follow me," Luke yelled out his window. "You
were right before, Callie. We need to go to the
southwest to get out. We'll get Adam and then
we'll go." The wind was much stronger, but Luke
couldn't tell if the smoke was any thicker. They had
been in it so long he was used to it now, adjusting
his breathing to take short, shallow breaths. His
hair was almost dry from dunking it in the pool.
When they got out of here, he was going to dive
into a real swimming pool and never get out.

"Stop before you get to those boxes. I want to
see if they're still working," Callie said, starting
up the golf cart.

"Okay." Luke waved at her and turned the truck

toward the main part of the camp. It was strange to be driving the truck. It was so much higher up in the air than the golf cart or the jeep. He glanced over at Theo. Theo was drinking another bottle of water, holding Tocho in his lap with his other hand.

"Are you still okay, Theo?"

"I guess so. Do you want some water? Callie put some in here."

Luke took a bottle with one hand, pulling the steering wheel too far with the other, making them lurch to the side. "It isn't as easy to drive as I thought it was going to be."

"I can tell. Remind me not to ride with you again until you pass driver's ed." Theo leaned out the window and looked back. "Callie's keeping up with you. She really can drive. She's pretty smart too."

"You don't want to make her mad, though. She doesn't forget easily." Luke turned the wheel too far to the left and the tire scraped the curb.

"Never mind," Theo said. "Don't talk; just drive."

Once they were away from the main buildings, Luke slowed the truck.

"We need to get off the road to go in the right

direction. It's going to be bumpy."

"Are you sure the truck is going to fit through the trees?"

"We'll make it fit. Hold on." Luke bounced off the road, trying to find the right speed to be able to maneuver around the trees. He ended up cutting back and forth to find room, running over anything small enough to fit under the truck. Every time he looked in the rearview mirror he saw Callie, crouched over the steering wheel of the golf cart, her eyes focused on the back of the truck.

Comet whined when Luke bounced the truck over a big exposed root, and Theo put up a hand to brace himself.

"How soon before we get to the defense system?" Theo asked.

"We're already past it," Luke said. "Callie didn't notice; she was so busy trying to follow me. I knew it would be off. It's going to make her mad when she finds out. She doesn't like it when I fool her."

Theo shook his head. "Remind me to stand back then."

"How bad can it be?"

It was bad. When Luke pulled up beside the

jeep and stopped the truck, Callie was right behind him. She leaped out of the golf cart and ran toward the truck.

"You liar! You liar! I hate it when people lie to me. How could you! You're just lucky it was off!" She stomped around, punching the air. "If you weren't the President's kid, I'd . . . I'd . . . I don't know what I would do, but it would be something terrible!"

"Luke! Adam's awake," Theo said, stopping Callie in midpunch.

Luke ran over to the tree where they had left Adam. He was struggling to sit up.

"Water," Adam croaked.

"Get some water, quick."

Callie gave Luke a bottle, and Luke held it up to Adam's mouth. Adam managed to swallow a little.

"Thanks," he whispered.

A roar drowned out everything, and when Luke turned to the sound he saw a massive wall of flame rise up to the east. He looked at Callie and Theo. No one needed to say anything. They helped Adam into the golf cart, and within seconds Luke had the truck started, driving away from the flames, Callie following. Luke drove as fast as he could, scraping trees on both sides, trying to see if the fire was visible in the rearview mirror.

"We're not going to clear that one!" Theo yelled. The side of the truck slammed into a tree and a mirror ripped off. Luke turned the wheel back and pushed on the gas, forcing the truck through the opening.

"We didn't need that mirror anyway," Luke said, trying to keep control of the truck.

As they moved to the southwest, away from both the fires, Luke thought the air felt a little clearer. The roar wasn't as loud. When he could see larger gaps through the trees, Luke knew the fence was close. He slowed the truck, not sure he would be able to see the fence in the dim light of the smoke-filled air. When he thought he caught a glimpse of it, he stopped.

"Now are you going to tell us what you're doing?" Callie asked, climbing out of the golf cart. "Whatever it is, I hope it doesn't take long." She looked back over her shoulder. "How much time do we have, Theo?"

"Not very much. We drove faster than it can spread, but it will catch up pretty soon. You'd better explain things quick, Luke."

Luke lowered the lift. "I do listen sometimes when my dad talks about ancient battles," he said. "The ancient Romans used battering rams all the time. We're going to turn the truck into a battering ram!"

Theo looked as if he would do anything to have a notebook in hand.

"Before you start pacing, Theo," Luke said, "I know what you're going to say." Luke started throwing the ropes down off the truck. "Electricity conducts through metal, so anyone inside when the truck hits would get a jolt of electricity. That's why I brought the two-by-fours. We'll tie down the steering wheel and then brace a piece of wood against the gas pedal and one on the brake pedal. We pull out the one on the brake pedal and let the truck go. No one has to be in it."

Theo paced. "Okay, I can picture that. Come on, let's help him." He climbed in the truck too. "What if the truck doesn't bring the fence all the way down? The fence looks strong."

"I know, but I've looked at the fence before. It's made to keep people out, and the fence sections are bolted on the outside of the supports so they won't push in as easily. We are coming from it the other way. The truck won't be able to knock it down completely, but that's okay. We're going to short out the fence."

"How?" Callie asked. "Wasn't it made to prevent that?"

Luke threw down the two-by-fours. "Like I said, the fence is designed to make it hard to get in here, and to give the Marines an edge if there were an attack. If someone tried to get in, the idea is that the fence would slow them down long enough to allow the Marines to counterattack. The fence isn't a perfect defense by itself. We're going to short it out with a chain." Luke picked up the sledgehammers and threw them out.

"I don't get it. Do we just throw the chain at it?"

"No, we attach the chain to the back bumper of the truck so it drags on the ground. Do you get it, Theo? It's just like when some insulation wears away on an electric train set and things short out."

"Yes, brilliant! When the truck hits the fence, the electricity will go through the truck and then the chain and then go to ground. It might short out the fence, especially if the wires are already damaged by the impact."

"Okay, whatever you say. We should stop talking about this and do it," Callie said. "What do we do first?"

"As soon as I get the truck positioned, Theo, you put the chain on the back bumper, so the metal can conduct the electricity. Here, take the creeper and the block and tackle out."

Luke backed the truck up as far away as he could from the fence and parked it so it faced between two support pillars. He hoped it was far enough back to pick up enough speed. It wouldn't make a dent if it just bumped into the fence. After a few attempts, Luke found the right sizes of boards to brace both the gas pedal and the brake pedal. Theo helped him tie the steering wheel in place.

"Are we ready?" Luke placed the brace on the brake pedal and then started the engine. He picked up the board for the gas and pushed it into place, nearly flooring it. The blast of sound surprised him as the truck strained to move forward. "You two stand way back when I pull out the wood on the brake pedal." Callie and Theo moved away.

"Wait!" Theo said, running back toward Luke as Luke was reaching his arm into the cab. "The truck is going to go forward so fast you might not be able to get your arm out of the way. We have to tie a rope around the board so you can stand far enough back and pull on it."

"You're right." Luke stepped back, a little shaky at how close he had come to potential disaster.

"We're going to have to turn the truck off to do this. You don't want to accidentally dislodge the brake."

Luke reached in and shut off the engine, telling himself he would never again think Theo worried about safety too much.

Once the rope was in place, Theo said, "I'm not sure this is such a good idea. You're going to have to yank on the rope and then drop it right away. If you hold on to it too long, it will pull you, because that two-by-four isn't going to come all the way out of the truck. It will get stuck somewhere."

Luke had pictured the two-by-four flying out the door before the truck moved, but now he realized Theo was right again.

"I got it," Luke said. "Move back." He started the engine again, and then he pulled hard on the rope, dropping it as he fell backward. The truck lurched forward and the wood caught in the door just as Theo said it would. The truck picked up speed, turning a little to the left. It still managed to crash into the fence between the supports, the front of the truck tipping up as the fence buckled. There was a crackling, hissing sound, and bolts of electricity raced down the truck, sparking and crackling. Then nothing.

"I think it worked," Callie said in a hushed voice. "I don't hear the humming anymore."

Luke picked up a stick. "Do you have any water left? Pour some on the end of this."

"We have lots of water left." Callie soaked the stick. "I'm not going to ask for a long explanation," she said with a grin.

"If the fence is still live, it will spark when it touches the water. Wood is not a very good conductor of electricity, so it won't hurt me." Luke came close to the fence. He knew he was right, but it was still hard to reach the stick out and touch it to the fence.

When nothing happened, Callie danced around them, grabbing Luke and kissing him and then moving on to Theo. Theo drew back and then stopped, letting her grab and kiss him too.

"Let's go," she yelled. "Last one over the fence is a rotten egg." She dashed over to the fence and started to climb across.

"Callie," Luke called, "we have some other stuff to do to get Adam out. We can use the sledgehammers to break down the outer fence, but we can't carry him to safety. He might be able to walk a little, but he can't outrun the fire."

Callie came back. She walked over to Adam and then came close to Luke. "Luke, Adam's unconscious again." She glanced at Theo and then back at Luke. "Did you ever think we should leave him?" she said slowly. "You know they must be sending more helicopters, and the fire is still coming." She pointed to the east, where a red glow rose above the trees, the crackling getting louder again. "It's coming closer. Why don't we get out so we can tell them where Adam is?"

"He wouldn't want you endangering yourself to save him," Theo said. "We should get out while we can. Let's go."

31

Netherworld

Luke looked at the two of them, clenching his fists. "I don't care what anyone would want me to do," he bellowed. "I'm sick of people getting hurt because of me, just because it's their job. For the last time, I am not leaving him! You go if you want. I have to get to work." He walked over and picked up the longest, thickest piece of rope, looping it around his neck, fighting back tears.

"We're staying," Callie said. "That was stupid of us. Just tell us what to do."

After Luke explained, Theo began to laugh so hard, he had to sit on the ground holding his sides. When he stopped laughing, he said, "I don't know how you came up with that, but it's so crazy, it might work."

"I'm glad you think it's so funny," Callie yelled. "It's more than crazy; it's ridiculous. Whoever heard of pulling a golf cart up in a tree and running it along a zip line over a fence?"

"No, it's brilliant," Theo said. "Once it's on the other side, we'll all fit in. We'll just drive to where we can find someone to help us."

"Hector's idea back at the front gate made me think of it," Luke said. "His plan wouldn't work as long as the electric fence was live, because a rope couldn't be tied high enough on the trees outside of the fence to support someone's weight coming straight across. They're pruned so you can't. But we don't want that anyway. I'm going to tie the rope around a trunk on the other side, lower to the ground. Now that the fence is partway down, the line will start high on this side and run down so the cart just clears the fence to the other side."

"A golf cart is too heavy. You can't lift it up in a tree." Callie wiped some sweat off her face.

"The block and tackle will lift a lot of weight," Luke said. "That's what it's made for, because with all the pulleys you can lift more than you could with just a rope. The heaviest part of a golf cart is the batteries, and there are six of them. We take them out and carry them over ourselves. Then we put the batteries back in on the other side. This rope is supposed to hold five hundred pounds. I know because Sal made us use this sort of rope when we built the tree house. A golf cart without the batteries probably weighs about five hundred pounds." He really didn't know how much a golf cart weighed, but he wasn't going to tell them that.

"Whatever you say." Callie sighed. "I'm too tired to think. What do we do?"

"I already know which tree I want to use on this side." Luke picked up the coil of rope, slung it over his shoulder, and then grabbed the sledge-hammer. "We need to knock a hole in the outer fence so I can find a good tree on the other side."

When he climbed up and over the electric fence, he felt his knee throb, but he knew he couldn't let it slow him down. Theo followed, and after a few minutes Callie came too.

"Let's see how hard it is to knock this down," Luke said, taking a swing. He put all his weight into it, but only one board cracked.

"Let me try," Theo said. Theo's swing punched

through and he kept at it, splintering the wood.

When enough pieces were broken, Luke said, "Let me get through so I can scout around. You two keep working until there's a big enough space to get Adam through."

Luke found an oak tree he thought would be strong enough, and then he realized where he was. He was outside the fence, by himself. Even though the woods were the same, it felt strange, like all the trees had grown bigger but he had shrunk. He put his cheek against the rough bark. What was Sal doing right now? Why hadn't he come to the back gate? Luke couldn't even tell how much time had passed; it seemed like hours and hours, but he didn't think they would still be alive if it had been that long. What was his father doing? Was Air Force One on its way back to Washington? Was his mom on her way home?

Taking a breath, Luke slung the coil of rope around to his back and climbed, trying to think only of getting to the branch he wanted. He was so tired he had to think about moving each arm and each leg one at a time, like he was controlling a puppet on a string. At the first fork he looped the rope around the trunk and tied it off. He fed out some of the rope, then started to make his way down, wishing he'd worn work gloves as the rope fibers burned against his hands.

On the ground, Luke fed out more of the rope and then made his way back to the fence. He saw the golf cart pulled right up to the edge, and Callie leaning over Adam. She was smiling and opening a water bottle again. Luke was amazed to see Theo reach out and take one of Adam's arms while Adam used the other to push himself off the seat.

"Hey, pal," Adam said to Luke. He swayed toward Theo, and Theo caught him, sagging under Adam's weight.

"Don't talk, Adam," Callie said. "Luke, we already took Tocho and Comet over and we're going to help Adam over the fence. It will be a lot easier than carrying him if he can do part of it himself. Get on his other side."

"Let me get rid of the rope first."

They shuffled forward, using the bent fence like a ramp, Adam with his arms around Theo's and Luke's shoulders, his weight nearly collapsing Luke's legs every time he took a step.

At the top of the fence, now about four feet from the ground, Luke said, "You're going to have to sit down, Adam, and turn around to swing yourself off the fence." Adam was drenched in sweat, and his breath came in shallow gasps. He nodded his head.

Theo and Luke jumped down first and positioned themselves so they could help. Adam managed to turn around, but when he swung off the fence he couldn't hold on. Luke and Theo tried to catch him, but Adam's weight brought them all to the ground.

Adam lay still and then opened his eyes again.

"We're almost there," Theo said. "Do you think you can crawl over here just a little ways?"

Watching Adam struggle to crawl was so painful Luke had to turn away. "I'm going back over," he said, picking up the end of the rope and swinging himself up on the fence. He noticed that the metal on the fence was getting warm.

"That should be far enough," Luke heard Theo say.

Back inside the fence, Luke picked up another rope and added it to the section he still held, staggering a bit under the additional weight of the thick rope.

"Next job," Callie said.

"Drive the golf cart right under that tree. I have to get the ropes up it so I can fasten the other end of the zip line and bring the block and tackle up."

When the golf cart was in place, Luke climbed on the front, reaching up to grab the lowest branch. He pulled himself up and swung a leg over, willing himself to go the rest of the way.

After he tied off the zip line, he dropped the other rope over the largest branch forking toward the fence.

"Callie," he said, looking down and seeing Theo as well, "both of you can get the batteries out and get them over the fence. Use the creeper like a cart, because they're heavy. You can push it right up to the bent fence section. I'm coming back down to tie up the block and tackle. I'll need your help to pull it up into the tree."

The block and tackle went up more easily than Luke expected, with all of them pulling on the other end of the rope.

"Hold this while I get back up there and secure it." As Luke went back up in the tree, he wondered why he used to think tree climbing was fun.

"Only one more time on this side," he said, when he finished tying off the pulley system. "I'm coming down."

He walked around the golf cart. "We need to tie up the golf cart like you're putting ribbon on a present, front to back and side to side, with a loop at the top so I can loop another rope to the zip line once we get it up."

"How is it going to move along the zip line?" Callie asked.

"Gravity should carry it across. I tied the other end lower than the end on this side. The weight of the golf cart should be enough to make it slide along the rope. I'm going to have an extra rope hang from it in case we have to pull it along." This was the weakest part of the plan. Luke didn't know if the rope would hold, but he didn't want Callie and Theo to know.

The golf cart did look like a present once it was tied up. It would be a present to them all if the plan worked. Luke didn't think he could even crawl away from here now, much less outrun a fire. He coughed. His mouth felt like the inside of a fireplace. It was getting so hard to breathe, he felt like he wanted to take big gasps of the smoky air.

"We need to lift it up by pulling on the other end of the rope," Luke said. "Once it's up in the air, we can wrap our end around the tree, and then you two are going to have to hold it while I get back up there and attach it to the zip line."

Getting the golf cart up, Luke started to talk to himself in his head. *Just a few more minutes to get this up, a few more minutes to get it across, a few more minutes to get everyone in, a few more minutes to get away; it will all be over in a few more minutes.*

"Hurry, Luke!" Callie called. "I see the flames coming this way. They aren't very far off." The heat was so great now, Luke's hands were slippery with sweat as he tied a loop around the zip line and through the rope loop on the golf cart.

"Let go of the rope and get across the fence," he yelled down. "If this doesn't work, take off running. Don't wait for me."

"It will work," Callie said. Luke didn't look down. He let go of the top rope; the golf cart slid. The rope sagged down and started to fray.

"It's not going to clear the fence," he whispered, watching the cart dip lower and lower as it slid. The cart started to tip, the weight of the engine unbalancing it.

Luke held his breath as the wheels just skimmed the top edge of the fence. The cart slid on down the rope until it came to a stop about two feet above the ground. The rope snapped and it fell with a thud.

"Yes!" Luke yelled, punching his arm up in the air and almost losing his balance.

"Get out of there, Luke!" Callie screamed. Theo was already lifting the batteries back into the battery compartment. Luke slid down the pulley rope. The front edge of the fire was around the bottom of the tree now, the dead grass and twigs burning like little sparklers. He stopped, feet from the ground, not wanting to go straight into the fire.

"Jump!" Callie cried.

32

The Golf Cart

Luke pulled on the rope so it started to swing, and when it came close to the trunk he bent his knees, using the tree to push himself forward. He jumped out as far as he could, just clearing the fire as it moved forward, not in a smooth line but more like water flowing in rivulets. Sparks landed on his hair and he smelled it singeing. He picked a path and ran, slapping at his clothes as sparks hit.

When he reached the fence, he bent down to scramble up it, jerking his hand away when he felt the metal. The fence was hot now. The soles of his sneakers stuck as he made his way up the fence and he knew they were melting. At the top, he leaped down, falling to his knees.

Everyone but Callie was in the cart. Adam, conscious again, was in the front passenger seat. He had one arm wrapped around one of the roof supports. Theo sat in the tiny back cargo area, holding both Comet and Tocho, filling up the whole space. Luke looked behind him. The fire rose over the fence like an enormous ogre rising up to get them.

"I'm going to hang on to the side," Callie yelled. "Let's go!"

Luke jumped in the driver's seat and pushed on the pedal. They jolted down the hill, Luke trying hard to keep the cart from tipping over. They hit a rock and Callie swung out and almost lost her grip, but Luke reached his arm out and caught her, feeling a wave of fear at the thought of her falling.

They continued on down the hill, weaving among the trees. Luke had never been in this part of the park before. It was rough and uneven, without any signs of a hiking trail. A large stand of pines came up in front of them, and Luke turned the cart to the left, trying to go around. The smoke was so thick he couldn't see more than a few feet in front of them. He swallowed and looked ahead, trying to push the panic down. In the thick smoke, the fire was an eerie reddish glow, cackling like a witch gone crazy. The smoke swirled around, patches of darker smoke wavering like ghostly figures, or maybe real ones ready to come for him.

Comet whimpered, and without thinking Luke reached back to pet him. Comet licked his hand.

The fear broke then, leaving only rage behind, rage at being afraid. Luke was sick of the fear, sick of it leaching the very breath out of him and dragging him down, as if he were being sucked into a black hole. He wasn't going to let it.

"We'll be okay," Luke said. "We'll be okay." He headed straight downhill.

"Luke, I'm scared," Callie whispered.

"Just a few more minutes," he said. "We'll be okay."

They reached a road, but it was running parallel to the fire. The way to the south looked clear for a short distance, but he didn't know if the road curved back toward Camp David. The flames were visible above the trees, leaping high into the sky. He was ready to drive across the road and plunge the cart into the forest on the other side when Callie yelled, "I see a helicopter." Luke stopped the cart and leaned out. Callie was pointing to the south. Luke saw the outline but couldn't hear the engine over the roaring fire. Taking a chance, Luke turned the cart in the direction of the helicopter. "We'll follow the road to the south and see if it buys us some time. Hold on." He floored the pedal and took off down the road, driving until the helicopter was almost on top of them.

"Everybody out," he said, stopping the cart and leaping out. "Callie, help Theo. I'll help Adam."

"Luke, something's wrong with Theo," Callie shouted, Comet in her arms and Tocho clinging to her shoulder. "I think he fainted or something."

Luke ran around to the other side. Theo was slumped over, almost falling out of the cart.

"Not now, not now!" Luke yelled, trying to pull Theo upright.

The helicopter hovered, the rotors stirring up the hot air. Luke looked up to see a soldier in a harness coming down a cable. The man dropped to the ground in front of them.

"Let's get moving, people," the soldier said, so calmly it seemed he didn't notice the fire behind them. "I'm going to have to take you all up by harness. We can't chance landing, because we don't know how fast the fire will move." He held out the harness to Luke.

"Mr. Brockett, you first."

"No, I'm going last. Take Theo and Adam. They're hurt."

"We don't have much time to argue," the soldier said.

"Luke, you've gotten us all this far. Just go," Callie said.

Luke took the harness and held it out to her.

"Adam and Theo go first. I go last." Luke moved back and crossed his arms.

The soldier looked at Luke and then said, "Okay, son, I'm not going to argue with you, because I want out of here. If you're going to be stubborn, at least help me get the harness on these people."

Once Theo was buckled in, Callie said, "Can you take the kitten too?" She set Comet down and unpeeled Tocho's claws from her hair. Luke could see scratch marks against her face.

The soldier just made an exasperated noise and took the kitten, signaling to someone above, and he, Theo, and Tocho rose in the air. Theo slumped in the harness, not moving. Through the smoke, Luke could see hands reaching from inside the helicopter. The soldier disappeared inside for a moment, then came back down.

"Mr. Brockett, my commander is up there yelling at me to grab hold of you and get you in this harness," the soldier said. "Now, do I have to do that?"

Luke moved back again. "We both know you can't get me in the harness unless I cooperate, and I'm not going to. I go last."

"It's no use arguing with him," Callie said. "Since he's the President's son, he thinks he should get his way all the time. He's spoiled, you know." She smiled at Luke.

"Okay, okay." The soldier sounded really angry. "I'm not going to chase you. When it's your turn, Mr. Brockett, I expect you to move fast. You are putting everybody in danger right now with your attitude."

The soldier moved to get Adam in the harness. Adam was conscious enough to stand leaning on the side of the golf cart until the harness was on.

When the two were in the air, Callie said, "You *are* being really stubborn, Luke."

"I know," Luke said. He didn't know why it was so important he go last; he just knew it was right. "I'm spoiled, just like you said."

The soldier was down again. "Hurry, young lady. We're almost out of time."

He'd snapped the last buckle of the harness on Callie when Luke felt the ground shift. Callie lost her balance and fell against the soldier.

"It's another earthquake!" the soldier yelled as Luke fought to stay standing. There was a sound like a train and the fire roared up through the forest, the flames billowing toward them, a blazing tidal wave of red. Sparks showered them, and Luke smelled more singed hair. Comet barked.

"Roll, roll," the soldier yelled, pushing Luke to the ground. "Your shirt is on fire!" Callie, still in the harness, fell toward him as the soldier hit at his shirt and then grabbed his side, rolling him back and forth. It all happened so fast, Luke couldn't make himself do anything; he just let the soldier move him around.

"It's out! Take hold of me." The soldier reached down and pulled Luke up. "We're all going up together."

Luke got one hand around the soldier's neck. Callie almost made them fall again as she reached down and picked up Comet. The dog yelped as she put him against her chest. They started to rise in the air, more sparks flying around them. The helicopter rose higher and the motion sent them swinging, first away from the fire and then closer to it. The flames were so hot, Luke thought they were all on fire. His eyes burned, but when he closed them he felt like his eyelids were melting.

Just when he thought he couldn't stand the heat anymore, he felt cool air on his face. They were up above green trees now, though he could see the fire to the east.

"Hold on just a few more seconds," the soldier said. The crank above them pulled them up right below the door to the helicopter, but then Luke felt a jerk.

"The harness!" the soldier yelled. Luke looked up. The harness strap hooked to the cable wire was singed black from the fire, and fraying. Sparks must have landed on it. "We're not going to make it. Drop the dog!" The soldier tried to use the hand not holding on to Luke to get Comet away from Callie, but the motion made Luke shift down, his grip loosening on the man's neck.

"No!" Callie said.

The soldier hoisted Luke up higher, wrapping both his arms around him. "Drop the dog or we're all going to fall!" Someone in the helicopter was making the crank move them up inch by inch. Luke could see another soldier above them leaning out the door.

"Move Comet toward me, Callie," Luke said. "I'll take him." Callie shifted Comet out to her side.

"You're not going to drop him, are you, Luke?"

Luke looked up to see the fraying mesh above them.

"No, let go of him." In one motion Luke took his hands away from the soldier's neck, hoping the soldier wouldn't lose his hold on him, and grabbed Comet, heaving him up in the air, pushing with all his strength as he launched his dog toward the man in the helicopter. The man reached out and grabbed Comet under one leg, pulling him in.

Then Luke felt hands taking hold of him and he was inside the helicopter.

"He's burned," Luke heard the soldier say. Luke's eyes were watering so much he couldn't see very well.

"Don't touch the burn until we get him to a hospital," another man said. "Luke, are you hurt anywhere else? Just nod or shake your head." Luke shook his head. "Can you sit up? You'll breathe better upright." Someone put his arm around Luke, supporting him while Luke pushed himself up. "That's a good sign. I'm going to put an oxygen mask over your face," he heard the man say. "It will just make you more comfortable, nothing to worry about. Breathe normally."

The effort of sitting up exhausted Luke so much, he just held still while someone put a mask over his face. When he took a breath, the air inside the mask felt cool against his mouth and he relaxed, wanting to lie down.

"Let's get him in a seat."

Another voice said, "Let me help you, Mr. Brockett." Luke opened his eyes just as a soldier practically lifted him into the seat right behind the pilot. Luke turned and could make out people in the back bent over Adam and Theo. The same soldier put Callie in the seat next to him. Luke blinked his eyes until he could see better. Callie already had Tocho in her arms.

"Can you ask someone back there if Theo, my friend, will be okay?" Luke said to the soldier.

The soldier gave him a thumbs-up and went to the rear of the helicopter. Luke looked out the window at the mass of smoke to the east. He couldn't see Camp David at all.

When the soldier came back he said, "The doc

says it looks like a concussion, but his vital signs are good. He should be okay."

"Mr. Brockett, I have the President, uh, your father on the radio." The copilot handed Luke a headset.

"Dad! Dad!" Luke said.

"I'm here." The connection was full of static, but Luke could hear well enough. "Luke, are you all right?"

"I'm fine, Dad. What happened to Colonel Donlin and the agents at the gatehouse? Where's Sal? What happened to him?"

"Slow down. One thing at a time. Now that you managed to get the fence turned off, the emergency crews are on their way into the gatehouse."

"What about Sal? Is he okay?"

"He was . . . He had a run-in with a bear, of all things. One of his arms is slashed up pretty badly, but he'll be okay."

Luke didn't know whether to laugh or cry. "Can I see him?"

"As soon as the doctors give the okay. I'll see you in a few minutes."

"Bye, Dad." He pulled off the headset, and someone took it from him.

Luke closed his eyes and then he felt something being pressed into his hand.

"I forgot to give you this," Callie said. "I brought it from the ranch."

He opened his eyes to see a silvery bright gleam against the grime of his hand.

"Wow, that's a great galena," Luke said. "I don't know if I've ever seen one with such a nice color."

"It's yours," Callie said. "Next time you come back to the ranch, I'll show you where I found it. Maybe we'll find some more."

"That would be great," Luke said, closing his hand on the stone.

33

The White House

Luke watched the incoming helicopters from an upstairs window of the White House. "It's incredible that they never goof up," he said to Comet as he scratched behind the dog's ear. The Marine One helicopter always landed in exactly the right spot on the South Lawn, the pilot bringing the tires down precisely in the middle on the red metal disks laid out on the grass.

"The trainees practice over and over without any passengers on board," his dad said as he came into the room. "And if they can't do it right, they don't get promoted to pilot." He put a hand on Luke's shoulder. "I'll be home tonight, but I probably won't see you. I hear you haven't been eating much. Anything wrong?"

"I'm not very hungry." Luke wasn't very much of anything, and he hadn't been since the fire. The doctor who treated his burns told him it would be a while until he felt himself again, and to tell someone if he had nightmares or trouble sleeping. He hadn't had any problems, but he couldn't get away from the numb feeling that enveloped him like a cocoon.

It had been a week since the fire, and four days since the funeral for Isabelle. Before they left for the service, Luke's mom had told him what to say to Isabelle's parents, things like what a good person she was and how she had done her job so well. He was glad his mom had given him lines to speak, because he couldn't have found the words on his own, and he knew his dad was expecting him to play his part well. He pretended he was just saying something he memorized, like an assignment, so he wouldn't break down and cry. The crying was left until he was alone.

Colonel Donlin and Grant were both still hospitalized, but the doctors were optimistic. It was strange: They had survived because their injuries kept them down on the floor, where there was enough oxygen to keep them alive, and enough of the stone building left standing to shield them. They were also fortunate the area around the gatehouse was mostly grass, thin from the drought, and cut short to meet Camp David's standards. It would take time to rebuild the damaged parts of Camp David. Luckily the fire had followed an erratic path, splitting apart and going completely around some sections, while burning up others.

Comet growled. He always did the instant the helicopter touched down, because he hated all helicopters. Luke guessed the dog thought they were some sort of giant bird invading his space. A Marine sergeant opened the helicopter door, lowered the steps, and marched off, pivoting at the bottom, and then marching around to face the White House. He halted and stood at attention. Luke knew the sergeant would stay there, motionless, no matter how long it took, until his dad walked out to board.

"How are you doing with your temporary agents?" his dad asked.

"Okay, I guess," Luke said. He hadn't been paying much attention to them. Adam's concussion had been more serious than Theo's and was going to keep him off work for another two weeks. After that, it would be at least another month before he would be able to come back to Luke's detail. In the meantime, he would have another job. "Paperwork and a desk" was the way he had described it to Luke. Sal still had his arm in a sling, and was on medical leave.

"Sir, it's time to go," Christine said from the hall.

"Just a minute," Luke's dad said. "Luke, I know we haven't had much of a chance to talk, but I just wanted to let you know I'm very proud of you. You kept your head and thought through what needed to be done in the middle of a crisis. That's not something everybody can do."

"But it was all my fault! I didn't hold on to Comet and that made—"

"Stop, Luke; look at me. Accidents happen. No one blames you. I learned many years ago you can't go back and change the past, no matter how much you want to, so it's best to move on."

Luke didn't know how he was supposed to do that.

George Michelson came into the room. "Sir, we're ready."

"All right, I'm ready. Luke, I'll see you tomorrow."

He ruffled Luke's hair and then strode out of the room.

Luke turned back to the window. The sergeant on the lawn looked like a statue. Luke wondered what would happen if a fly landed on the man, or he had to sneeze.

"Surprise!"

Comet barked and Luke whirled around. Callie and Theo stood in the doorway, Adam behind them.

"What are you doing here?"

"Aren't you glad to see us?" Callie asked.

"Your mom arranged for Callie and me to visit you," Theo said. Luke was relieved Theo looked normal again.

"You should feel special," Callie said. "I put on a dress and everything."

"Uh, you . . . you . . . It's nice." She looked kind of odd wearing cowboy boots with a dress, but Luke decided not to point that out.

"I was in to pick up some forms"—Adam held up a briefcase—"when I saw these two at the security desk. I told the guard I'd bring them up and say hello. Everything okay with you?"

"Everything's good." Luke realized he actually meant it.

Comet bounded over to Callie and jumped up on her, making the pocket of her dress squeak.

"Callie!" Luke said.

"Please don't tell me you sneaked a kitten into the White House." Adam shook his head as if willing her to say no.

"Of course not. I think Tocho's already grown too big for my pocket just from feeding him for a few days." Callie pulled out a dog toy, a fuzzy rabbit that squeaked when she squeezed it. "I brought a present for Comet. He's not such a bad dog after all." She tossed the rabbit up in the air and Comet caught it before it hit the ground.

"That's a relief," Adam said. "The other agents would never let me forget it if they saw me escorting an unauthorized kitten off the property." They watched as Comet carried his captive under a desk so he could chew on it undisturbed. Adam checked his watch. "I think I'll leave you three to talk. I have a feeling I need all the rest I can get before I come back to work."

"Okay," Luke said. "See you soon."

After Adam left, Luke wasn't quite sure what to do, especially with Callie here. He hadn't had a girl visit him before, even though Callie wasn't like a regular girl. One of his temporary agents came in.

"Luke, your mother arranged for some ice cream to be sent up from the kitchen for the three of you. It's all set up in the dining room."

"Ice cream! Nice!" Theo said.

Luke was relieved. Even though he wasn't hungry, ice cream would keep Theo and Callie busy for a while. "I bet they sent up all sorts of toppings too," he said. "They know I like to experiment. Come on, I'll show you the way."

"You don't mean we're going to eat ice cream in one of the big rooms they show on TV?" Callie asked.

"No, we have our own dining room in the living quarters. Those rooms are only used for special occasions."

"That's good," Callie said. "So if I spill something, it won't matter, right?"

"Right," Luke said. "Comet, here, boy. Bring your rabbit."

The kitchen staff had outdone themselves. There were six kinds of ice cream all displayed in big bowls of crushed ice, and in front of those were dishes and dishes of toppings and syrups.

Theo filled a bowl up with cherry ice cream and then topped it off with crushed-up candy bars, bananas, and chocolate sauce, adding mounds of whipped cream.

"Callie, I just found out you are going to our school." Theo took a huge bite.

"I didn't know that," Luke said.

"You didn't know your mom arranged for me to get a scholarship?" Callie asked. "Hmm . . . I think I want strawberry with chocolate sprinkles and bits of mint cookie. Anyway, that's why I'm going there. My dad could never afford to pay tuition to a fancy private school. It seems weird I need a scholarship to go to seventh grade, and I'm probably not going to like it. My dad says I can still go back to the ranch if it doesn't work out."

"You'll like it. Won't she, Luke?" Theo took another bite, and a bit of candy bar fell to the floor. Comet shot out from under the table, dropped his rabbit, and licked it up. "They have lots of clubs and activities. Since you like photography, you should join the photography club."

"That might be fun," Callie said doubtfully.

"Luke and I really like the robotics club. Guess

what? I'm getting a robot kit tomorrow. My mom promised. Are you going to get a new one?" Theo asked Luke. The tree house had burned in the fire, along with the extra robot pieces they had left there. The snake-catcher robot survived the fire, but the microprocessor was too damaged to be used again.

"I haven't asked."

"You should. I'm sure you'll get one. You can help me with mine too. We can build a robot that walks, and then program it to talk."

"What would we make it say?" Luke asked. "Wait, I have an idea, a great idea! We could program it to stop when it came to a door and start again when the door opened. That way if we sent it down the elevator, it would come out by itself when the doors opened. The Secret Service agents would be really surprised." Luke was so excited he almost drummed on Theo. "Oh, and I know what else we could do. We could program it to say, really slowly, like the aliens in those old cartoons, 'Take . . . me . . . to . . . your . . . leader.' That would be so funny!" He took a quick breath of air. "But we'd need to see the agents' expressions. We could—"

"Hold on," Callie said. "I can already tell the

two of you are going to get into trouble with all your crazy ideas."

"Since when have you ever worried about getting into trouble?" Luke laughed. "Besides, it won't just be the two of us. We'll need you to help us. You know, come up with the practical bits to make our plans work better."

Callie frowned. "If I help you, will you promise not to boss me around?"

"I don't boss you around. You're the one who's bossy."

"I am not!"

"Guys, guys, the ice cream is melting. Why don't we eat it while we're planning how to do this?" Theo asked.

"Good idea," Luke said. He decided he was hungry, and nothing would taste better than a bowl of chocolate ice cream with chocolate sauce and bits of milk-chocolate candy bars, all topped off with fresh raspberries.

Author's Note

While this story is fiction, Camp David is a real place. Presidents and their families have used it since the 1940s as a way to vacation away from the pressures of living in the White House. Even on vacations, though, a President's safety and that of the First Family are still major concerns. Like Luke Brockett in this book, children of U.S. presidents have their own teams of Secret Service agents who accompany them almost everywhere. The children often spend more time with the agents than with their parents.

The agents are trained to guard their charges under any conditions, no matter how strange. When Amy Carter, the daughter of President Jimmy Carter, was living in the White House, she attended an animal show where an elephant named Susie charged toward her, so a Secret Service agent picked her up and carried her over a fence to safety, breaking his hand in the process. Agents also sat in the back of Amy's fourth-grade class every day and went with her to the playground for recess. Older presidential children must have agents go with them to college, where new friends and potential dates are often screened to determine if there is a safety risk. *Protecting the President*, by Dennis V. N. McCarthy, and

Standing Next to History, by Joseph Petro, both former Secret Service agents, were major sources for this story.

The layout of the real Camp David and the security systems there today are not public knowledge. All those aspects in this story are fiction. Almost all of the historical detail, however, is factual. The swimming pool was indeed built over the old bomb shelter, and the expense to reinforce the roof of the shelter was reported to cost as much as the pool itself. The one fictional addition is the boarded-up bomb shelter steps. I am indebted to W. Dale Nelson, the author of *The President Is at Camp David*, for his very detailed history of the facility.

Acknowledgments

Major thanks go to my agent, Caryn Wiseman, and my editor, Barbara Lalicki, for taking a chance on an unknown and unpublished writer.

My family played many parts in bringing this story to life and so deserve many thanks. I couldn't have done any of this without my husband, Dean, and his unflagging support of my writing over the years, and his willingness to try to come up with an answer to every question, no matter how strange. This is a good place to apologize to him as well, for all the research I do on the internet about subjects that probably put me on a few watch lists. Thanks go to my children, Garret and Hope, who not only suggested ideas, but were willing guinea pigs and helpers in my quest for accuracy; to my brother, Kim Garretson, who helped add some excitement to the story; to my sister, Terri Bruch, who managed to catch some glaring errors; and to my niece's husband, Ryan Gillmore, and my brother-in-law, Chris Bruch, who patiently answered my questions.

I also want to thank Dr. Julie O'Connell and Shelli Caskey for their help with my animal questions. And finally, thanks to Michael Neff, who made me realize I needed to push my imagination as far as it could go.

WILDFIRE
RUN

Q&A with Dee Garretson

Behind the Scenes: The Secret Service

A Sneak Peek at Dee's Upcoming Novel, *Wolf Storm*

Q&A with Dee Garretson

Dee Garretson tells us about the writing process, her inspiration for *Wildfire Run*, and what she would do if she were President!

Luke's status is an important part of *Wildfire Run*. How did you decide that the hero of your action-packed adventure would be the son of the President?
I like to write about characters whose lives are very different from my own, and the son of a U.S. President is about as different as can be! Presidential kids lead such an odd life. On the one hand, they have incredible privileges and experiences: flying on Air Force One, living in the White House, and getting to go to exotic places would be great. On the other hand, it would be awkward and annoying to have Secret Service agents following you around all the time, going with you to school, and being around when you hang out with friends or go to a movie. It would also be frightening to have to worry about all the dangers you and your family might face. I thought such a contradictory sort of life would make an interesting story.

What kind of research did you do for *Wildfire Run* about Camp David and about the techniques the three friends use to escape it?
Researching Camp David was like putting together a puzzle when you can't find all the pieces. There isn't much information released about the place, because the secrecy helps keep it secure. I spent quite a bit of time at the library reading biographies of past presidents who had been there. I also read memoirs of Secret Service agents, and I did find one book

3

devoted to the history of Camp David. When I found that, it was like finding a bit of treasure!

When it came to the techniques the friends use to escape, I relied on help from people in different professions who could give me answers to all my questions. It was a long process of first thinking up different obstacles, and then making sure actual kids could figure out how to overcome them. I also relied on my own children. They helped me build and program the same robot that Luke, Callie, and Theo use in the story, and I also asked them questions about what they would do in certain circumstances.

Luke, Theo, and Callie are very different. Which one are you most like?

I've got parts of both Callie and Luke in me. Callie is practical, and so am I. I like to figure out the best, least complicated way to do things. I am also crazy about animals, and I might have been the kind of kid to sneak a kitten into Camp David. Luke and I have traits in common, too. Like Luke, I have so many ideas and subjects I'm interested in that it's hard to concentrate on one thing. I would also rather be outside than inside, and I don't sit still for long. I'm least like Theo, but I admire people with his type of personality. I try to be organized like he is—it just doesn't always work.

You founded the website kidsadventurebooks.com. What is it about adventure books that you love so much? Did you always want to write an adventure book of your own?

I've always loved adventure books, because when I read I'm usually thinking, what if that were me? What would I do? Could I be brave enough to take on something dangerous?

I also love them because so many are set in places I've never been. That's why I like fantasy and science-fiction stories, as well as adventure stories set in the real world. It's so much fun to imagine what it would be like to experience the story. For a long time, it didn't occur to me to write down the stories I made up in my head. I didn't even think about being a professional writer. I wanted first to be a veterinarian, then an artist, and then a doctor. I didn't think my stories would interest anyone else. It took a long time to convince myself my ideas might be worth writing down.

Can you describe your writing process? Did you tell your own kids about the story as it was developing?

I start with trying to think of an exciting story I would want to experience only if I could somehow magically get inside it. After that, I come up with characters who fit the story, and try to make them ones I want to spend a lot of time thinking about. I don't want a character I dislike, unless the character is supposed to be a villain, because I wouldn't want to be stuck carrying an annoying or unlikeable character around in my head for months!

My kids are a great help with my writing. I know what interests them and I bounce ideas around with them. They help me name characters, and we often build models or try out plot ideas together. There is a section in *Wildfire Run* in which Luke, Callie, and Theo crawl through a shield made of jeep doors. My kids and I built a cardboard model made to the exact size of real doors to make sure that part of the story worked. I think they enjoyed it. I know they enjoyed my attempts at making plum dumplings to get the food right in my next book, *Wolf Storm*, and both of them are excited about helping me create a new book trailer. They also keep coming up with locations for the setting of another book, so that they could hopefully travel with me to do research!

If you were President and had a private vacation retreat, what would you want there? Would it be more like Camp David or more like the ranch Callie is from?

I love forests so if I had my own vacation retreat, it would be more like the actual Camp David than a ranch. I'd probably do some extra work on the hiking paths, though, to make them a little more exciting. It would be great to be able to cross rope bridges, go behind waterfalls, and climb up rock walls during a hike.

I made up the ranch where Callie lived because I do like the idea of having horses and room for lots of animals. I had a pony growing up and miss not having much opportunity to ride now. The first stories I ever wrote were horse stories. In the past, several presidents have kept horses at Camp David, so I'm sure there are still stables there, or if not, I'd have more built. A great swimming pool would be a necessity, and if I could add buildings, I would put in a library and a big conservatory full of plants and birds, so that in the wintertime it would seem like summer inside. I could go on, but that would almost make another book.

Behind the Scenes: The Secret Service

The name Secret Service sounds like it comes straight from a made-up story about a mysterious and exciting organization. In reality, it's an actual part of the U.S. government and just as secretive and intriguing as it sounds.

The members of the Secret Service are a specialized, highly trained group of people who willingly put their lives on the line to protect the U.S. President, his family, and other government officials, including VIPs from other countries when they are visiting the United States. The agents also have another job that is less publicized—protecting the nation's money supply from counterfeiters who try to pass off fake money as real currency. The organization was originally formed for this purpose, long before the country realized our presidents needed to be protected.

There are Secret Service offices in every U.S. state, as well as Puerto Rico, Guam, and in sixteen other countries. To apply for a job with the group, an applicant must have either a four-year college degree or three years' experience in law enforcement. Many, many people want to work there, so the more education or experience a person has, the more likely he or she is to be hired. Not all employees work directly protecting government officials. There are scientists, engineers, forensic specialists, and photographers in the Secret Service, too. Everyone who works for the organization has to be able to get a Top Secret clearance, which means they are deemed trustworthy enough to see classified information.

Once a person is hired for a special agent position, they go through training in areas such as firearms, marksmanship, emergency medical techniques, financial crimes detection, and water survival. There is a special training facility with a street and buildings like a movie set, where agents practice different scenarios that might occur, such as an ambush or other kinds of disasters. Trainees even have to practice escaping from a helicopter submerged in the water, just in case such an incident might occur.

A uniformed division of the Secret Service helps guard federal buildings and sites the President, Vice President, or other protectees are planning to visit. This division has a canine unit with dogs who are trained to detect explosives. They use a breed called the Belgian Malinois, dogs somewhat similar to German shepherds. Each dog stays with his or her handler twenty-four hours a day, like a member of the handler's family.

The Secret Service is always evolving as technology and threats change, but to maintain its effectiveness it keeps its operations highly confidential. To find out more about it, check out the organization's official website at http://www.secretservice.gov.

Chapter 1

THE LAIR

CARPATHIAN MOUNTAINS, SLOVAKIA, EASTERN EUROPE

Snow lay thick in the ruins of the castle walls, drifting over the best hiding places. The creatures who lived there didn't know the broken stone was the work of men. The stench of humans had disappeared centuries ago. Occasional hikers who came to picnic in the summer never stayed long enough to embed their own scent. Those times the creatures faded into the shadows, waiting patiently, knowing the humans wouldn't linger. Now, in the depths of what seemed an endless winter, summer warmth was just a trace of a memory and food was so scarce, it was time to venture farther afield before starvation set in.

Chapter 2

PROWLING

ICE PLANET EARTH SET, SLOVAKIA

The wolf Boris pushed his nose into Stefan's hand, its breath warm against the coldness of Stefan's fingers. Stefan tried to keep his hand very still, just in case the animal mistook his fingers for a chew toy. The animals in the movie were supposed to be highly trained and perfectly safe, but still, a wolf was a wolf. "Um, good boy," he murmured. "Nice wolf." Boris licked his hand like he was testing its flavor potential. "Trust me," Stefan said. "You'd rather have wolf kibble."

Jeremy Cline, who played his younger brother, shifted around, bumping into Stefan. "Sorry, your sleeve is tickling my face," Jeremy said.

"Hold still," Raine Randolph hissed. Raine was supposed to be playing their demanding sister, and from what Stefan had seen, it wouldn't be a stretch for her. They were already behind in the filming schedule for the day because of Raine's fit about the placement of the metal barrette things in her hair. She'd made the hair person shift them around several times. Then she had complained about the boots she wore, because they didn't make her look tall enough. He knew famous stars were used to getting their way, but he hadn't expected a thirteen-year-old could get away with acting like she was queen of the world.

"The ramp is slippery! There isn't enough room," Jeremy said. The three of them, along with two wolves and the actor playing their grandfather, were crammed into the doorway of a mock spaceship, waiting for the director to tell them what to do. It wasn't even a whole spaceship, just one side of it, held up by wooden supports. Mark, the director, had explained it was too expensive to build a complete one for the exterior shots, but Stefan was still a little disappointed.

"I just want close-ups on the kids' faces," Mark said to one of the cameramen. "Capture their emotions when they see all the snow and the desolation." He turned toward them. "Okay, kids. Let's get in the mood here. You're the first humans to come back to a post-apocalyptic Earth in eons. You're devastated you were forced to leave your parents and your own planet behind, and you don't know how long you're going to be stuck on this frozen world. Earth is now in another ice age, and you don't know what you're facing. Up until the spaceship door opens, the reality of it hasn't hit you. All we want today is the looks on your faces when you realize just how bad the situation is.

"We'll put the ramp back up before the camera rolls. Then, when I call for action, the ramp comes down, and Stefan, you're out first with Boris. Raine and her wolf, Inky, go to your right, and Jeremy to your left. Jeremy, we'll get an establishing shot of you with your wolf later. There just isn't room on the ramp for all of them. The wolves will move to their marks, those bits of cloth fastened to the ramp, so follow their lead." He gestured to the other cameraman. "Alan, I want good coverage of the lead wolf early on. Boris is going to rock the screen when we do his fight shots. He is one mean-looking wolf when he snarls." As if to disprove that, Boris licked Stefan's hand again and wagged his tail.

Stefan laughed and patted the wolf again, then acted like he was grabbing an invisible microphone. "You ain't nothing but a hound dog," he sang. Boris wagged his tail harder.

Jeremy giggled. "I recognize that one. It's the guy named Elvis who wore those sparkly white suits. My grandmother loves him." Raine didn't laugh. She hadn't laughed at Stefan's Elmo the Muppet imitation either, when they were having their costumes checked. She'd given him that "you're so immature" look girls perfected early on.

"Can you teach me how to do imitations?" Jeremy said, looking up at Stefan.

"Um, maybe," Stefan said. Jeremy was already showing too many signs of latching on to him, tagging after him and asking questions. The last thing Stefan wanted was some kid following him around all the time. He got enough of that at home from his little brothers. On his very first movie, he was going to take advantage of being on his own.

"Hold still boys, please, so we can finish the light check," Mark said. "Stefan, remember, you're supposed to be the oldest. Without your father here, you're the leader of the group. The troops with you are loyal to your family and expect you to be in charge, so look confident." Stefan liked the idea of being in charge of his own troops, even if none of them were actually on set yet. It was easy enough to imagine a whole squadron of men behind him in the spaceship.

"Get the snow off the ramp before you take it up," Mark told one of the crew as he brushed the snow off his beard. The crew were all quickly turning to snowmen. The snow had been falling steadily, fine powdery flakes that coated people and surfaces within minutes. Stefan was glad he didn't have to be one of the people shoveling snow. That was usually his job back home, so it felt nice to watch someone else have to do it.

When the ramp was clear, Mark motioned for it to be taken it up. "Okay, let's try this."

Behind the raised ramp, Stefan closed his eyes, trying to envision being in a real spaceship. He heard Mark's muffled voice from the other side call, "Roll sound." Then silence. "Roll camera. Action!"

The ramp came down with a soft thump on the snow and Hans, the wolf trainer, signaled the animals to move. Stefan knew he wasn't supposed to look at the trainer, but the signal distracted him, and for a split second his eyes shifted to the man.

"Cut!" Mark said. "Raine, that was perfect. Stefan, maybe a little less dismayed, please, and don't look at Hans. You are afraid, but you don't want anyone to know. Put your hand on Boris's neck; the wolves are the symbol of your family's power and he's also your best friend. Hold on just a minute. I want the camera shifted a bit."

Stefan tried to think of how someone would look acting brave and confident. His mind went blank. He stared up into the mountains surrounding the set. At least it didn't take too much acting for the dismay part. The set was in the middle of nowhere, a nowhere buried in several feet of snow. When he'd finally gotten the word he had been cast, and that they were going to start filming on location in the country of Slovakia, in Eastern Europe, he'd had to look it up on a map. The set was at an old ski resort in the Carpathian Mountains that had been closed for years. The whole place was stark and forbidding, a flat plateau halfway up a mountain, surrounded by other mountains and accessible only by a narrow switchback road cut through a cliff.

The muscles on Boris's neck tensed underneath his hand and the wolf strained toward the snack truck. Stefan was puzzled. The array of food was incredible, bagels and chocolate and yogurt and granola bars and fruit, but he didn't think there was anything there a wolf would want, no platters of deer burgers or sheep steaks.

"Let's try again," Mark said. "Once the ramp is up, get the snow off their hair and faces so it looks like they have just arrived."

This time when the ramp came down, Stefan moved forward and glimpsed something peering around the side of the snack truck. It looked like one of the wolves but was too shaggy, and it was gray. All the set wolves were black, or at least all the ones he had seen. Had one of the spare ones gotten loose?

"Cut. Stefan, don't look like you see something," Mark said. "Remember, there's nothing but snow and ice."

Boris growled, his attention focused in the direction of the food truck, and Stefan could tell he had seen the animal too. The animal ducked behind the truck and Boris crouched down like he was getting ready to take off after it.

17

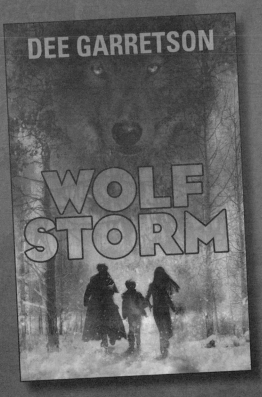